Felix co...**time he'd felt an attraction this strong.**

And he *wanted*. So badly that it shocked him to the core.

Daisy Bell was seriously striking when she wasn't hiding behind her chief mechanic clothes. Surely men told her all the time how beautiful she was?

And that look in her eyes, quickly masked, told him that the attraction was mutual. There was a definite connection between them.

So what were they going to do about this?

Mixing business and pleasure was a mistake he didn't make. Ever. But Daisy Bell really tempted him to break all his rules. Tempted him to reach out and twirl a strand of her hair round his forefinger, to see if it felt as soft and silky as it looked. To kiss her, to find out if her sea-green eyes turned the colour of jade when she was aroused.

She looked at his mouth, and he knew from her expression that she was thinking exactly the same thing. Wondering what it would be like. How he would taste. How electric it would be between them…

GOOD GIRL OR
GOLD-DIGGER?

BY
KATE HARDY

MILLS & BOON®
MODERN
Heat™

First published in Great Britain 2010
Harlequin Mills & Boon Limited,
Eton House, 18-24 Paradise Road, Richmond, Surrey TW9 1SR

© Pamela Brooks 2010

ISBN: 978 0 263 87733 5

Harlequin Mills & Boon policy is to use papers that are natural, renewable and recyclable products and made from wood grown in sustainable forests. The logging and manufacturing process conform to the legal environmental regulations of the country of origin.

Printed and bound in Spain
by Litografia Rosés, S.A., Barcelona

Kate Hardy lives in Norwich, in the east of England, with her husband, two young children, and too many books to count! When she's not busy writing romance or researching local history, she helps out at her children's schools; she's a school governor and chair of the PTA. She also loves cooking—see if you can spot the recipes sneaked into her books! (They're also on her website, along with extracts and stories behind the books.)

Writing for Mills & Boon has been a dream come true for Kate—something she'd wanted to do ever since she was twelve. She's been writing Mills & Boon® Medical™ Romances for nearly five years now, and also writes for Modern Heat™. She says it's the best of both worlds, because she gets to learn lots of new things when she's researching the background to a book—add a touch of passion, drama and danger, a new gorgeous hero every time, and it's the perfect job!

Kate's always delighted to hear from readers, so do drop in to her website at www.katehardy.com

Recent titles by the same author:

Modern Heat™

TEMPORARY BOSS, PERMANENT MISTRESS
PLAYBOY BOSS, PREGNANCY OF PASSION
  (*To Tame a Playboy* duet)
SURRENDER TO THE PLAYBOY SHEIKH
  (*To Tame a Playboy* duet)

Medical™ Romance

THE DOCTOR'S LOST-AND-FOUND BRIDE
FALLING FOR THE PLAYBOY MILLIONAIRE
  (*Brides of Penhally Bay*)
THE CHILDREN'S DOCTOR'S SPECIAL PROPOSAL
  (*The London Victoria* duet)
THE GREEK DOCTOR'S NEW-YEAR BABY
  (*The London Victoria* duet)

For Gerard, with all my love

CHAPTER ONE

THIS had to be some horribly realistic nightmare. It couldn't be happening. It *couldn't*.

Daisy closed her eyes and pinched her arm.

When it hurt, the sick feeling in her stomach intensified, and she opened her eyes again to face the facts.

Someone really had broken into the fairground museum. Several people—and pretty drunk, too, judging by the number of smashed bottles around the gallopers and the vomit sprayed nearby. Yobs who'd thought it would be a laugh to cut off the horses' tails and spray-paint obscene graffiti along their sides. And they'd used the café as a coconut shy and lobbed stones through the plate glass, wrecking it.

Daisy had always been practical and could fix almost anything, but she couldn't fix this—at least, not fast enough. No way could she open the fairground today. It would take days to sort out this mess and make it safe for children and families again.

Who on earth would do something like this? It was completely beyond her. Why would anyone want to wreck such a beautiful piece of machinery, an important piece of heritage, just for kicks?

With shaking hands, Daisy grabbed her mobile phone and called the police to report the damage.

When she'd finished, she called her uncle. She hated having to call him on his day off—the day when *she* was supposed to be in charge and opening up—but this had stopped being a normal Sunday. And she wasn't the only one who had a huge stake in the museum; Bill had given it half a lifetime.

'Bill, it's Daisy. I'm so sorry to ring you at this time on a Sunday morning, but…' She swallowed hard, not knowing what to say, how to tell him such awful news.

'Daisy, are you all right? What's happened?'

'Vandals must've got in last night. I don't know how.' Daisy knew beyond all doubt that she'd locked up properly the night before. 'But there's a lot of broken glass and they've damaged the gallopers.' She bit her lip. 'The police are on their way. We'll have to stay closed for at least today, probably tomorrow as well.'

This would have to happen so early in the season. As they ran the museum on a shoestring, this was going to put a major hole in their budget. It could all be fixed, but it would take time, and they'd have to pay the insurance excess, which wouldn't be small. Not to mention the missed takings until the fairground was back in action. Disappointed tourists might be put off ever coming back to the museum, and they'd tell their friends, too, who would then shelve their own planned visit. And that would hit future takings.

Without a decent amount of visitors through the gates, there wouldn't be money for their planned restoration programme. The ride she'd managed to rescue last autumn would have another year for rust to creep through it, another year that might mean it was too late to save it. So instead of having a working set of vintage chair-o-planes that would absolutely thrill their visitors they'd be left with a heap of useless scrap metal. All that money wasted, and she'd been the one who'd stuck her neck out and persuaded Bill to buy it in the first place. So much for proving that she could take over when Bill retired in a couple of years. She'd spent money they should've kept as reserves in case of situations like this.

'The police want statements from me, obviously, as I'm the one who discovered it. But they said they'd like to talk to you as well. I'm sorry, Bill.'

'All right, love. I'm on my way,' Bill reassured her. 'I'll be there in twenty minutes.'

'Thanks. I'll put up some signs saying we're closed today and then start ringing round the staff. See you in a bit.' Daisy slid the phone back into her pocket and stared at the gallopers, the Victorian roundabout that her great-grandfather had built, complete with its original fairground organ. Part of her wanted to go over to each of the mutilated horses in turn and hug them, tell them that everything was going to be OK. Stupid, she knew. Apart from anything else, it might damage any evidence the yobs had left behind. And the horses were wooden, had no feelings. But she'd grown up with them, could remember riding them as a toddler, and it felt as if someone just had smashed something from her childhood and trampled on it.

She'd spent ten years of her life helping to build this place up: ten years when she'd taken a tough course in mechanical engineering, having to justify herself to her parents, to her tutors, to the other students on the course. Ten years when she'd had to persuade people that she was doing the right thing. Half the time they'd thought they knew better, and Stuart had even made her choose between the fairground and him.

Not that it had been much of an ultimatum. Any man who wanted to change her and stop her doing what she loved wasn't the right man for her. She knew she'd made the right choice, turning him down. The right choice for both of them. He was married with small children, now, children that he regularly brought to the fairground.

Funny how he could see what she saw in it now.

But it was too late. Even if Stu hadn't been married, she wasn't interested any more. When her next two boy-friends had turned out to be from the same mould as him—wanting her to change and be a girly girl instead of a skilled mechanic—she'd decided to cut her losses and concentrate on her work. At least here she'd been accepted for who she was—once she'd persuaded the older volunteers that she was a chip off her grand-mother's block. She'd proved that she could listen and work hard, and that she was good at her job.

She'd fixed the notice to the gates stating that the fair-ground was closed due to unavoidable circumstances and was sitting at her desk, working her way through the list of volunteers, when Bill and Nancy walked in. Bill was grim-faced.

'I can't believe this,' he said when she put the phone down. 'I'd like to get my hands on whoever did it and give them a bloody good hiding.'

'I'd rather stake them out, smear them in jam and leave them to the wasps,' Daisy said. 'Or maybe use the road-roller and squish them. How could they do it? I mean, what did they get out of it?' Her fists balled in anger and frustration. 'I just don't understand why anyone would do something like that.'

'I know, love.' Bill hugged her. 'All that work everyone's put in, wrecked.'

'And all the people who were planning to come here today—they'll be so disappointed.' She dragged in a breath. 'Maybe I should ring Annie.' Her best friend was the features editor of the local newspaper. 'She'll know how to get it onto the radio news-desk, so it'll save some people a wasted journey.'

'Good idea, love,' Nancy said.

'I've been ringing round and telling everyone to stay at home today,' Daisy explained. 'So far, everyone's said to call them when the police say we can start clearing up and they'll come in and help.'

'We're lucky. We've got a good crowd.' Bill sighed. 'You call Annie, and Nancy and I will keep going with the volunteers' list.'

'I'll put the kettle on first,' Nancy said. 'I know we've got milk in the office fridge; I'll go and get some more later, or when they let us back in the café, but it'll keep us going for now.'

Annie turned up in the middle of the police interviews with chocolate cake and a photographer. 'Cake because it makes everyone feel better, and photographs because this is probably going to make the front page. And you're perfect for it, Daze.'

'You want photographs of *me*?' Daisy asked, mystified. 'Why? I mean, doesn't the scene out there speak for itself?'

'You know what they say—a picture paints a thousand words,' Annie said. 'And you're really photogenic, Daze—plus you wear your heart on your sleeve, so everyone's going to be able to see how upset you are. Your face will get a huge sympathy vote.'

'I don't want sympathy. I want my fairground back the way it should be,' Daisy told her.

'I know, hon, and it will be,' Annie soothed. 'The local radio and television will pick up on this. You can get the word out through them and the paper that you're closed for the rest of the week, and it'll also remind people that you're here. With any luck, you'll get tons more visitors than normal next weekend because they'll want to come and rubberneck.'

Daisy grimaced. 'Annie, that's horrible.'

'It's human nature,' Annie said. 'You know, that policeman over there keeps giving you the eye. Give him a smile.'

'Annie!' Daisy looked at her best friend in disbelief. The fairground was in trouble and Annie was thinking about fixing her up with a man?

'Daze, working here you don't exactly get to meet many single men, let alone men below the age of fifty,' Annie said, sounding completely unrepentant. 'Seize the day. He's very cute. And he's definitely interested.'

Daisy blew out a breath. 'Well, I'm not interested in *him*, thanks very much.'

'Mind if I go and have a chat to him?'

'Do what you like, as long as you don't try to fix me up on a blind date with him.' Daisy scowled. 'Not everyone wants a life partner, you know.'

'And you're happy with just your cat?' Annie asked, looking unconvinced.

'Yes, I am. Titan's good company and he's not demanding.'

Annie scoffed. 'Not demanding? This is the cat who has a plush bed in every room of your house and a taste for fresh poached salmon.'

'OK, but he's still not as demanding as a man would be.' Her cat didn't want her to change and be *more feminine*. He loved her for herself, not for who he wanted her to be. 'Though he's not very happy with me right now because I've locked him in my office to make sure he doesn't get broken glass in his paws.' She frowned. 'Why are we talking about this? Annie, I know you're happy with Ray—and I'm really happy for you—but I'm fine as I am, really.'

'Hmm.' Annie looked at her. 'Right. I'm going to chat to that policeman, because I need some information for my copy. And while I'm gone Si's going to take a picture of you looking distraught.'

'I'm not sure it's a good idea to have my picture in the paper.'

'Tough. I've already cleared it with Bill. He says you're prettier than he is, so you're doing it.' She smiled.

Daisy sighed. 'You're such a hard-nosed journo.'

'Annie Sylvester, Super-Hack: that's me.' Annie gave her a hug. 'And once the police say we can start clearing up I'll give you a hand dealing with the glass and scrubbing all the paint off. I'll give Ray a ring and he'll come and muck in, too.'

'Thanks. I owe you,' Daisy said.

'Course you don't. That's what best mates are for. You'd do the same for me.' She paused. 'Have you called the rest of your family yet?'

'No.' Daisy lifted her chin. She was perfectly capable of running her own life, and most people realised early on that she was the kind of person who fixed things efficiently and without a fuss, but her family still insisted on treating her as the baby, the one who had to be bailed out of things. It drove her crazy, even more so than their insistence that career progression and earning a good salary was more important than job satisfaction. If she called them, of course they'd come—but she'd be living up to all their prejudices. 'Bill, Nancy and I can manage.'

'Sometimes,' Annie said softly, 'you can be too proud, you know.'

'Let's agree to disagree.' Daisy sighed. 'Look, I love them, and we get on fine—most of the time. But I don't want a lecture or an I-told-you-so speech, and that'd be the price of them helping. You know that, too. So it's better to keep things smooth and keep them away from it.'

'If you say so, hon. But wouldn't it be better that they heard the news from you than saw it on the front page of the paper tomorrow morning?'

Daisy knew her best friend was right. 'OK. I'll talk to them tonight, I promise.' When she'd fixed as much as she could.

The rest of the day seemed to be spent giving statements and making cups of tea while they waited for the scene-of-crime team to finish gathering evidence so they could start fixing the mess the vandals had left. By the time the light had gone, the café windows were boarded up temporarily, the glass had been swept up and they'd made a start on removing the graffiti.

But Monday morning brought more bad news. 'The insurance company says we're not covered,' Daisy told Bill, settling on the edge of his desk. 'Apparently vandalism's been excluded from our policy for three years.' She sighed. 'It seems they changed our policy terms when Derek was ill, and nobody picked it up at the time.' Derek was Bill's best friend and their insurance broker.

'So we have to pay for the damage ourselves?'

She nodded grimly. 'They can recommend a glazier, but we'll have to pay the full cost of repairs.'

'And plate glass costs a fortune.' Bill muttered a curse under his breath and shook his head. 'I know we can't afford *not* to fix the café, but we can't afford to fix it, either.'

She dragged in a breath. 'Because I talked you into buying the chair-o-planes.'

'Love, they were a bargain, and we would've kicked ourselves if we'd missed the chance. It's not that.' Bill sighed. 'The way the stock markets have gone, my investments are worth practically nothing now, even if I cash them in—and you know as well as I do we run this place on a shoestring. If we go to the bank and ask for a loan, they'll laugh us out of the office because we couldn't pay it back.'

'Not from the museum takings,' Daisy said. 'But there's my house.' The two-up-two-down terraced house her grandmother had left her. 'I can talk the bank into giving me a mortgage to release some of the equity.'

'On the salary you draw from here, they wouldn't lend you a penny.' Bill shook his head. 'And I wouldn't let you get into debt for this anyway. No, love.'

'It's my heritage as well,' Daisy pointed out. Her uncle had often said that she was the child he and Nancy hadn't been able to have. 'Your grandfather, my great-grandfather.' She took a deep breath. She'd been thinking about Annie's words since yesterday. Maybe her best friend was right. It had been a bit unfair of her to tell her family by text message last night and then switch her phone off so they couldn't get hold of her. She hadn't given them the chance to help because she hadn't wanted to deal with the way they saw her. But maybe it was time she swallowed her pride, for the sake of the fairground. This was something she couldn't fix on her own; they did need bailing out. 'We could ask Dad, Ben, Ed and Mikey to help. They'd chip in, because it's their heritage, too.'

'No. Ben has a young family to think about, Ed and Mikey have huge mortgages and your dad's about to retire.' Bill sighed. 'His investments are in the same state as mine.'

And there was still the fact that Daisy's family saw the fairground as Bill's whimsy, which in their view was stopping Daisy from having a proper career. Which was why she avoided talking to them about it.

Bill looked grim. 'We're going to have to get a backer outside the family.'

'Who's going to invest in a steam-fairground museum in a recession?' Daisy asked.

'The prices of steam engines are rocketing—no pun intended,' Bill said, with a nod to the model of Stephenson's Rocket on his desk. 'So right now investors will see their money as being safer here than in shares.'

Daisy shook her head. 'Investors always come with conditions attached. And they won't see this the way we do, that we're conserving our heritage. They'll want to see big returns on their money—they'll want a hike in entrance fees and more stuff in the shop. And what if they decide to pull out? How would we raise the money to buy out their share?'

'I don't know, love.' Bill looked bleak. 'We could sell the showman's engine.'

It was worth a small fortune, but it was also the last

engine that Bell's had ever made, and Daisy had spent four years working on its restoration. 'Over my dead body. There has to be another way.'

'Short of winning the lottery, or discovering that fairy godmothers are real, I doubt it, love. We'll have to take on a partner.'

'Or a sponsor, perhaps.' Daisy sighed. 'I'll stick the kettle on. And then we'll work out what we can offer a sponsor, make a list of all the local businessmen and divvy up the calls between us.' She hugged him. 'We'll find our silver lining.'

Felix picked the phone up without taking his eyes off the spreadsheet. 'Gisbourne.'

'Oh good. I'm so glad you're there, Felix.'

Felix sighed inwardly; it served him right for not checking the caller display first. Now his sister was going to nag him instead of leaving a message on his answering machine. Which meant he couldn't fast-forward it, or delete the message unheard and tell a white lie about his answering machine going wrong. 'Good morning, Antonia.'

'Mummy says you're weaselling out of the house party this weekend.'

Typical Antonia: she always came straight to the point. 'Sorry, sweets. Can't make it. I'm busy at work.'

'Come off it,' Antonia scoffed. 'You're perfectly capable of going to the house party and sorting out your business stuff first thing in the morning, before anyone else in the house even thinks of getting up.'

True. But it didn't mean that he wanted to do it.

'Mummy really wants you there.'

'Only because she's lined up yet another suitable

woman for me.' Felix sighed. 'Look, Toni, I'm not interested in getting married. I'm *never* getting married.'

'Don't try and con me that you're not interested in women. I saw that picture of you in the gossip rags the other week, with a certain actress draped all over you. Or are you going to tell me you're just good friends?'

'No. It was a…' He compressed his mouth and shook his head in irritation. 'Toni, for pity's sake, you're my little sister. I am *not* discussing my love life with you.'

'The lack of it, more like. Your women never last more than three dates.' She sighed. 'You know that Mummy just wants you to be happy. We all do.'

'I *am* happy.'

'Settled, then.'

'I have a nice flat in Docklands and a successful business. That counts as settled in most people's eyes.'

'You know what I mean. Settled with *someone*.'

'I'm allergic to women with wedding bells in their eyes.' He paused. 'I just wish our mother would get off my case.'

'If you hadn't got cold feet over poor Tabitha, you'd be safely married off by now and Mummy would be happy,' Antonia pointed out.

Maybe, but Felix certainly wouldn't have been. His marriage would have been an utter nightmare. For a moment, he wondered if he should've told his family the truth about Tabitha. But then they would've been even worse, treating him like a victim, crowding him and pitying him, and he would've hated that even more than he hated their constant attempts to fix him up with someone. On balance, it was better that they thought him a heart-breaker who just needed the right woman to tame him.

Except he didn't need anyone. He was perfectly happy with his life as it was: with a job that fulfilled him, and dating women who understood right from the start that he wasn't looking for long-term, just for fun. Because he was never, ever going to put himself in another situation like he had with his ex-fiancée. He would never let his heart be that vulnerable again. 'Maybe,' he said.

'Come on, Felix. It won't be so bad.'

Oh yes, it would be. His mother must have introduced him to every single blonde with long legs in the whole of Gloucestershire, because she thought he liked leggy blondes.

Well, he did.

He just didn't want to get married to one. Didn't want to get married to *anyone*.

'Toni, I really am busy, so I'll call you later, OK?'

She sighed. 'OK. But you'd better, or I'll ring you.'

'Message received and understood. Bye, sweetie.'

He put the phone down and leaned back in his chair, frowning. Time to find a cast-iron excuse to avoid his parents. The sad thing was, he would've enjoyed a weekend in the country, had it been just the family there. He liked his parents and his sisters, and even his brothers-in-law were good company. But Sophie Gisbourne had decided that her only son needed to be married, so she always insisted that weekends at their Cotswolds estate would involve a house party. And every time she invited a 'suitable' woman to be his partner at dinner—with the subtext being that she would be a suitable partner for life as well.

Sometimes Felix thought that his mother had been born two hundred years too late. She would've made the perfect Regency mama, brokering marriage and offering advice to friends. But in this day and age it was just infuriating. He went into the small kitchen and made two mugs of coffee, adding sugar to his PA's mug before returning to the office. 'Here you go, Mina.' He noticed that his PA looked uncharacteristically upset. 'Are you OK? What's wrong?'

Mina flapped a hand at him. 'Don't mind me, it's silly.'

There were tears in her eyes. He perched on the edge of her desk. 'Talk to me. Someone's ill? You need time off?'

'No, nothing like that. Mum sent me this.' She handed him a sheet of newspaper that had clearly been folded neatly and sent through the post:

VANDALS PUT FAIRGROUND MUSEUM IN A SPIN

'She used to take me there when I was little. It's a really magical place.' Mina's mouth compressed. 'I can't believe vandals would wreck it like that.'

Felix skimmed down to the picture of a woman sitting on an old-fashioned fairground ride, looking heartbroken. There was something about her, something that made him want to see what she looked like when she smiled.

Which was crazy. You couldn't make decisions on the basis of a photograph of someone you'd never met. He wasn't that reckless.

Besides, she wasn't his type. For the last three years he'd dated mainly tall blondes with long legs, plus the occasional redhead. But petite and brunette was definitely out: it would remind him too much of Tabitha.

But it seemed that the fairground needed rescuing.

That was his speciality: rescuing businesses before they went to the wall. And this was a business with a difference, something that might give him the challenge he felt that his life had lacked lately. It wouldn't hurt to take a look.

When he'd finished reading the article, he looked at Mina. 'Do you know the Bells?'

She shook her head.

'Can you get me the manager's number?' He smiled at her. 'This looks as if it could be an interesting opportunity.' And if he checked the place out for himself at the weekend, that gave him a valid excuse to avoid his mother's latest 'suitable women' onslaught without hurting her feelings.

Just perfect.

CHAPTER TWO

'SO THAT'S US,' Bill said with a smile. 'Well, me, anyway. You really need to meet my number two.'

Daisy Bell: the woman from the photograph, according to the article. Deputy manager of the fairground.

Felix was annoyed with himself for being so keen to meet her. For all he knew, she could be married or involved elsewhere. And he wasn't in the market for a relationship anyway.

But her face had haunted his dreams for the last week, and his heart rate speeded up a notch at the thought of finally meeting her.

'She's supposed to be here, but she's obviously forgotten the time,' Bill said.

How on earth could she forget a meeting that might make the difference between the museum being a going concern or heading straight for bankruptcy? This really didn't gel with the picture of the devastated woman in the paper. Or had it been a set-up? Drag in a pretty woman with tears in her eyes to give a human dimension to the piece and the saps would be flocking here in droves, wanting to protect her and invest in the fairground…

No, he was being cynical, letting his past get in the

way. William Bell seemed genuine enough. And Daisy had been dressed in trousers and a plain shirt, not a floaty dress and impractical heels. She wasn't the frivolous, frothy type that Tabitha had been. Just because Daisy was petite and brunette, like his ex-fiancée, it didn't mean that she shared the same personality traits: shallower than a puddle and a liar to boot.

But, now he'd started on that train of thought, he found it hard to stop. Why wasn't she at this meeting? Maybe the fairground wasn't really that important to her. Or maybe she didn't pull her weight, and her uncle put family loyalty before sound business practice and let her get away with it because she batted her eyelashes at him and told him he was her favourite uncle. Well, Felix was good at pruning dead wood and giving more able people a chance to prove themselves. If he was going to invest in the museum and turn the business around, and Daisy turned out to be a liability, he'd give her her marching orders. Very, very quickly. Pretty or not.

'It's going to be quicker to fish her out of the workshop,' Bill said. 'And I can show you round a bit at the same time.'

Felix's expectations hit a new low as they reached a single-storey building with breezeblock walls and a corrugated-iron roof. What was Daisy doing in the workshop—chatting up the mechanic when she was supposed to be working?

But as Bill opened the door Felix could hear someone singing—a female voice, giving a surprisingly good rendition of 'I Can See Clearly Now'.

'I thought as much,' Bill said with a wry chuckle. 'Her work's going well and she's lost track of time. You can always tell, because she sings. It's when things go badly that she's silent.'

'What's going well?' Felix asked, mystified.

'Work on the engine.' Bill looked puzzled. 'Didn't I tell you she's my chief mechanic as well as my number two?'

'No.' Felix blinked. It hadn't been on the website, either, or in the article. 'Mechanic?'

'A word to the wise: she's a bit touchy about sexism,' Bill said. 'And she gives as good as she gets—it comes from having three older brothers.'

'Right.' Felix mentally readjusted his picture of Daisy. A mechanic and a bit touchy: to him, that suggested a woman with muscles, cropped hair, probably a nose ring or a tattoo, and an attitude to go with it. But the woman in the photograph hadn't looked like that. She hadn't been wearing a skirt, admittedly, and her hair had been pulled back from her face, but she hadn't looked butch.

He was definitely missing something here. But what?

When they entered the building he could see feet sticking out from under an engine, wearing Doc Martens—bright purple ones. Each one had a stylised white daisy painted on it.

His mental picture took another shift. He could hear his mother sighing and saying, '*Most* unsuitable.'

Oh, for pity's sake. He was too old to rebel against his parents. He was thirty-four, not fourteen.

But he had a feeling that, with footwear that unusual, Daisy Bell herself would turn out to be equally unusual. And she was the first woman who'd intrigued him this much in a long, long time.

A large ginger cat was curled on top of the engine. 'Tell her she's got visitors, lad,' Bill said.

To Felix's surprise, the cat leapt down from its perch. A couple of seconds later, he heard a bang, followed by 'Ow!' and the singing stopped.

'Daisy. It's half-past ten,' Bill called.

'Oh, blimey. Tell me he's not here yet and I've still got time to tidy up?'

There was a grating sound—something rolling over concrete, Felix guessed—and then a woman emerged from under the engine.

The woman from the photograph.

She was wearing an oversized engine-driver's cap that covered her hair completely, an extremely shapeless and unflattering—not to mention dirty—boiler suit, and her face and hands were covered in oil. Face to face, she looked younger than he'd expected, though the newspaper report hadn't mentioned her age. She was in her very early twenties, he'd guess: too young and inexperienced for her position as Bill's second in command.

She couldn't be more than five feet four.

Not blonde, and not long-legged. Completely not his type. But the second that Felix met her sea-green eyes he felt as if there was some kind of connection between them. He couldn't define it, but it was there, zinging through him.

'Actually, love, he was early,' Bill said. 'Felix, this is my niece, chief mechanic and number two here, Daisy Bell. Daisy, this is Felix Gisbourne.'

Oh, no. Why hadn't she guessed that Bill would bring the man to meet her if she wasn't in the office on time? And why on earth hadn't she thought to ask someone to come and fetch her at least half an hour before Felix Gisbourne was due, so she could at least have greeted him with a handshake? Daisy wiped her hands on a rag, inspected them briefly and knew they didn't pass muster.

'Sorry.' She grimaced. 'I don't want to cover you in oil. Better take the handshake as read.'

'Of course.' Felix gave her a polite nod.

He was nothing like Daisy had imagined. She'd expected someone nearing his fifties, not someone who looked as if he was around her own age, almost thirty.

And he was the most gorgeous man she'd ever seen. Tall, with dark hair, fair skin, dark grey eyes and a mouth that promised sensuality—the kind of looks that made women take a second glance at an ad in a glossy magazine, even a third. He could've made a fortune as a model.

Maybe he had been a model at one point. He certainly knew how to dress. His suit looked as if it was made to measure; it was teamed with a white shirt, sober tie and shoes which Daisy guessed were handmade and Italian. His outfit looked as if it cost more than the salary she drew each month.

He was absolutely immaculate—flawlessly groomed, clean shaven, and those shoes were polished to a dazzle. This was a man for whom appearances really mattered. The kind of man, she thought with an inward grimace, who'd expect the women he associated with to wear designer dresses and spend hours at the hairdresser's and beauty salon—which was so *not* her. She revised her earlier thought about Felix being a potential investor in the fairground. No way would a man who dressed so fastidiously muck in, in case he got his hands dirty. If he insisted on being anything more than a sleeping partner in Bell's, it wasn't going to work.

'Are you all right?' Bill asked.

'Yes. I just hit my head when Titan smacked me in the ear.'

Felix stared at her, as if he was wondering whether he'd been transported into some strange parallel-universe. 'The cat smacked you in the ear?'

'It normally means he's hungry or someone wants me,' Daisy elaborated. 'If I'm working on one of the engines, I don't always hear people come in. So they tell him to fetch me. He kind of thinks he's a dog. Or maybe a human, I'm not sure.'

A second later, the cat leapt from the engine onto her shoulder; absent-mindedly, she scratched behind his ears and he began to purr.

'Or Captain Flint?' Felix suggested, the corners of his mouth tilting.

Long John Silver's parrot. Daisy's smile was genuine for the first time. If the man had a sense of humour, it would take the edge off his pristine appearance—and it meant that maybe she could work with him. 'I've been trying to teach him to talk, but I'm afraid he's sticking with "meow" rather than "pieces of eight".'

'Daisy, would you show Felix round for me?' Bill asked.

'Course I will.' She looked at her uncle, narrowing her eyes slightly. He really didn't look that well. She made a mental note to have a word with Nancy and find out what Bill wasn't telling her about his health. Maybe it was just the worry about the fairground and whether their new visitor was going to invest in them or consider a big sponsorship deal. She could identify with that; she hadn't slept particularly well for the last few nights, either.

So she'd better put on a good show when she took Felix round the site, because she had no intention of letting her uncle down, or the part-time staff and volunteers who'd stood by them for years. If getting Felix Gisbourne to invest in them meant schmoozing, then she'd schmooze to Olympic gold medal standard.

Gently, she lifted the cat from her shoulder and set him back on the engine. 'We're going walkies. See you in a bit, OK?'

Titan purred.

'I'll bring Mr Gisbourne back to the office when I've shown him round, Bill.'

Bill smiled at her. 'Thanks, love.'

When Bill had left the workshop, she turned to Felix. 'What would you like to see first, Mr Gisbourne?'

'Felix,' he corrected. 'I prefer informality.'

'With that suit?' She clapped a hand to her mouth in horror as soon as the words were out. So much for the promise to herself to schmooze the guy. Why had she opened her mouth? 'Sorry. Forget I said that. Please,' she added belatedly.

'Whatever. Just walk me round and tell me what I'm looking at,' Felix said.

'OK. First off, this is a working museum, so our collection here is original rather than replica. But we believe that it's better for them to be used than just moulder away in glass cases while people look at them and think, "So what?" We want people to enjoy them, just like they have for the last hundred or so years. To get the real experience of an old-fashioned fairground.'

'You have rides dating from the 1800s?' he asked, sounding surprised.

'Yes. The gallopers date from 1895.' She shrugged. 'But I imagine you saw them in the paper.'

He nodded. 'Have they found whoever did it?'

'Not yet. Though, when they do, I'd like to have them under my command for a week,' Daisy said.

'So you could teach them a lesson?'

'It depends what you mean by lesson. When I saw

what they'd done, I admit I was furious. But when I'd calmed down a bit, I realised that if they're the kind who enjoy smashing things up, it's a fair bet they've grown up where nobody around them respected anything and they've learned to value nothing. If they worked for me, it'd give them a channel for their energy, and they might learn that they have a talent for something. It'd give them some self-respect—and that's the first step to being able to respect others.'

'So you'd let them off without punishment?' Felix said.

She spread her hands. 'Chucking kids in jail won't solve the problem—if they're stuck somewhere without an outlet for their energy, they'll brood and get more resentful, and they'll lash out as soon as they're out again. I want to show them that there's another way. Give them an interest and a stake in things. They're not going to destroy something they've spent time building—they'll want to protect it.'

He nodded. 'So you see the good in people.'

His face was impassive; was he saying that was a bad thing? Maybe it was, where business was concerned. 'Look, I'm not naïve enough to look at things through rose-coloured glasses, but seeing the good in things is a lot healthier than being cynical and believing that everyone's out solely for what they can get.'

'Indeed.'

'There's good and bad in everyone. The trick is finding how to maximise the good and minimise the bad.' She stopped, realising that she was getting carried away. 'Anyway, you didn't come here to listen to me on my soapbox. You want to see what we have here.' She took him round each ride, explaining their history as she did so. 'All the ones before 1935 were built by our family's firm. Though I couldn't resist the 1950s dodgems when we had the chance to buy them.'

Felix asked lots of questions as they walked round; each one seemed to be more critical than the last. By the time they reached the last ride—Daisy's favourite, the old switchback gondola—she'd had enough of his blatant criticism, and her intention of schmoozing him dissolved. She faced him, folding her arms. 'You seem to have a problem with just about everything I've told you, and I get the impression you think that Bill and I are amateurs. Let me tell you, he's run this place for nearly thirty years, and I've been working here for ten of them. He does a damn good job and you're judging him unfairly.'

'I'm assessing the business. It's what I do—and I'm good at it,' Felix replied, looking completely unfazed.

'This is what *we* do, and we're good at it,' Daisy countered, lifting her chin and wishing that she was six inches taller and fifty pounds heavier. If she were five feet ten and hefty, maybe he'd take her seriously.

'You might be a brilliant mechanic and understand everything to do with how the rides work and their history, but your business sense leaves a lot to be desired—and so does Bill's. There are lots of areas where you could be making money and you're not taking advantage of them, and you're definitely not using your assets to their full potential. That's why you don't have the money to cope with any setbacks, such as the vandalism. Your margins are way too tight.'

'This is *heritage*, Mr Gisbourne,' she said frostily.

'Felix,' he corrected.

Daisy deliberately didn't repeat his first name. 'The whole point of this place, Mr Gisbourne, is to make our heritage accessible to people. There are so few of these rides left, and even fewer of them are in working order; quite a few of those here were just left to rot, and we've rescued them and restored them.'

'Without enough money to run the place, you're not going to be able to make it accessible to people or afford the restoration costs. You'll go under. So you need to compromise.'

'That's why we're looking at sponsorship deals.' It was the whole point as to why he'd come to see them, wasn't it? To see what they could offer him and what he could offer them?

His eyes narrowed as he looked at her. 'You're not a woman who compromises easily, are you?'

Daisy thought of her ex-boyfriends and how the last three had tried to change her. If a man couldn't accept her for who she was and wanted to make her into a different person, someone she wasn't, then she wasn't interested. And the same went for her business. If the price of his investment was changing Bell's, making it all about the money instead of all about the heritage and fun, then she wasn't interested. If she had to, she'd take a part-time job to earn extra cash that she could feed into the fairground, to give them a breathing space until they found a sponsor who understood where they were coming from. 'I'm glad you realise that.' She lifted her chin a fraction higher. 'And don't be fooled by my name. I'm not a delicate little flower.'

'Daisy.' He tipped his head on one side. 'You're right. "Boots" suits you better.'

'Boots?'

He indicated her Doc Martens. 'And then there's the Cockney rhyming slang.'

Daisy roots: boots. She knew that. Although normally she loved puns, and adored tormenting her brothers with them, it annoyed her that Felix was being clever with her. She was about to say something tart when he spoke again.

'Have dinner with me at my hotel tonight.'

It sounded more like an order than a request, raising her hackles higher still. Why did he want to have dinner with her anyway? Was he trying to come on to her?

'A working dinner,' he clarified.

She could feel the blush staining her cheeks; clearly he'd worked out what she was thinking. Well, of course he hadn't been coming on to her. Men like Felix Gisbourne dated glamorous women who wore high heels and nail polish and earrings and expensive hairdos. He wouldn't be interested in the likes of her.

Besides, she wasn't interested in him as anything more than an investor. Couldn't be. The fairground was too important.

'Sure. I think Bill's free, too.'

'Actually,' he said, 'I was thinking just you and me. If you've been working as his number two for as long as he says you have, then you'll have the answers, and I won't have to drag him away from his family.'

Another assumption: that she didn't have anyone in her life to be dragged away from. Then again, he was right, so there was no point in arguing; she had no plans to spend her evening with anyone other than Titan.

'By the way,' he added, 'the hotel isn't really a jeans and boiler suits place.'

For a moment, she thought about telling him to get lost. In a truly pithy manner.

But then she thought of Bill, and the people who

depended on them for jobs, and forced her temper to simmer. 'Just tell me where and when to meet you.'

'Seven o'clock.'

He named a hotel five miles away, on the coast, the poshest one in the area; its restaurant had two Michelin stars. And it wasn't really within cycling distance—not with a skirt on, anyway—so she'd better organise a taxi. 'That's fine,' she said coolly. 'I'll see you at seven.'

His smile did weird things to her stomach. Oh, this was bad. She had to ignore the surge of attraction. Even if there hadn't been a business deal in the way, they were too different for it to work, because she wasn't suitable girlfriend-material.

'I'll look forward to it, Boots.' He sketched a salute, following up with another of those devastating smiles. She'd bet he knew the effect it had on women. 'I'll find my own way over to Bill.'

'I'll take you.'

'You're busy. I wouldn't want to disturb you.'

Too late. He already had disturbed her.

'*À bientôt*,' he said softly. 'Seven o'clock. Don't be late.'

Like she had been for their meeting this morning? That had been an aberration, she thought. As Felix Gisbourne was about to find out.

CHAPTER THREE

DAISY headed back to the workshop and grabbed her mobile phone. She speed-dialled her sister-in-law, willing Alexis to be there; she almost sagged with relief when the line connected and the answering machine didn't kick in.

'Lexy? It's Daisy. I need your help.'

'Sure, hon. What's up?'

Before she'd had children, Alexis Bell had been a make-up artist—a seriously good one. If someone could make a silk purse out of the sow's ear Daisy knew herself to be, it would be her sister-in-law. 'I need a makeover. And I need it, um, right now.'

'Excuse me? Am I hallucinating, or have you been drinking?'

'Neither.' Daisy explained the situation.

'He said *what*?' There was a dangerous edge to Alexis's voice.

Daisy repeated it.

'When are you meeting him?'

'Seven.'

'Get over here by half-past five and we'll sort it.'

'Thanks, Lexy. I owe you.'

Daisy just about managed to concentrate on her work for the rest of the day. At ten to five, she collected her bicycle from the back of the workshop, and Titan jumped gracefully into the wicker basket on the front, settling onto his cushion. She cycled home, fed the cat, picked up some fresh underwear, then called at the village shop just in time to pick up some flowers for Alexis before cycling over to Ben and Alexis's house. She was grateful that her oldest and favourite brother had decided to settle in the next village; it made life much easier.

Alexis greeted her with a hug. 'They're lovely, hon, but you didn't need to buy me flowers. I'm going to enjoy glamming you up.'

Not too much, Daisy hoped.

'So where are you going?'

Daisy named the hotel, and Alexis whistled. 'Right. Go and have a shower and wash your hair. I,' Alexis told her firmly, 'will deal with the rest. Luckily, you're the same size as me.' She grinned.

'I'm really grateful for this,' Daisy said humbly.

'If you're that grateful,' Alexis said, moisturising Daisy's face and then drying her hair, 'you'd let me do this more often.'

'It'd be wasted on the fairground.'

'When you're in chief mechanic mode, yes, but not when you're doing talks to schools. Though we'll argue about that later. As well as the fact that you really hurt Ben last week. If you'd called him, you know he would've come straight over and helped you clear up.'

Daisy shifted uncomfortably. 'I'm sorry.'

'You're too proud. And I bet Annie told you to call him.'

'Yes.' Daisy sighed. 'OK, take it as read that I'm a

horrible woman and I don't deserve your help. But, please, just make me look *girly* enough for tonight.'

Alexis hugged her. 'You're not horrible. I love you and so does Ben. I know he doesn't agree with your career choices, but he's learning to lump it—and he really would've helped out if you'd given him the chance.'

'And treated me like a baby.' Daisy couldn't help glowering.

'Honey, you're his little sister. And he's a bloke— he's hardwired to do the overprotective big brother thing, so you're just wasting energy if you fight it. He's not going to change. But, if it makes you feel better, he tells me you're better at fixing things than he is—and yes, I know he doesn't tell you that. That's men for you. Now, sit still and close your eyes.'

Given the array of cosmetics on the table, Daisy was feeling just a little nervous. But she sat still and let Alexis paint her face and finish her hair. Then she changed into the dress and low-heeled court shoes Alexis lent her, which was followed by a speedy lesson from her sister-in-law in how to walk like a model on a catwalk.

'Right. You can look in the mirror now,' Alexis said.

Daisy barely recognised herself as the petite, curvy woman whose hair was a mass of shining waves.

'This is really me?' She blinked. 'Blimey, Lexy. You're even better than I thought you were. Thank you so much.'

At that moment, the front door opened. Ben did a double-take. 'Who are you and what have you done with my little sister?'

'Ha, ha.' Daisy scowled at him.

'Daze, you look amazing. For you to wear a dress and let Lexy do your face, he must be special.'

'I'm not going on a date,' Daisy said through clenched teeth.

'Dressed like that?' He spread his hands. 'No way. It has to be a man.'

'Yes, and it's *business*. So don't you dare breathe a word to Mum, or I'll tie you to a tree and wax your chest. Slowly.'

Laughing, Ben held up his hands in surrender. 'Why on earth did the parents call you Daisy? They should've called you Godzilla.'

'Well, excuse me, I have to go home and beat my chest before I book a taxi.'

'You can't cycle home in that dress.' He looked at his wife and then at Daisy. 'I'll stick your bike in the back of the car and drive you.'

'I can manage,' Daisy said, with dignity.

'Yes, but you don't have to.' He sighed. 'You're so ridiculously independent.'

'Because I hate you treating me as if I'm a baby.'

'Well, you *are* my baby sister. OK, OK, I know.' He held his hands up in surrender again. 'So what's the business?'

She told him.

'Are you sure about this? Because if this guy thinks you're part of the deal…'

'He doesn't,' she cut in gently. 'And you don't have to look after me, Ben. I'm a big girl now.' She kissed him, leaving him a perfect lipstick-imprint on his cheek. 'Though I appreciate you watching my back.'

'Hmm.' He looked faintly embarrassed. 'Why don't you borrow the MG, Daze? It'll save you waiting for a taxi. I'll drop your bike back at yours, and you can bring my car back tomorrow.'

'You'd trust me with your car?' She knew how her brother felt about his old classic car.

'Sure. You understand what's under the bonnet. You'll treat her as she deserves.'

Daisy swallowed the lump in her throat. Was this Ben's way of telling her that he saw her as an adult after all? 'Thanks, Ben. I love you.'

'Good.' He smiled at her. 'I would ruffle your hair, but then Lexy would kill me for messing up her hard work. Go knock his socks off, kid. And if he says a word out of line—'

'I'll tell him my favourite brother's bigger than he is and will come and sort him out,' she teased, and hugged him again, before hugging Alexis, too. 'See you later. And thanks for the support. You two are wonderful.'

She drove to the coast. Ben was right, driving the MG did make her feel like a million dollars, but at the same time her stomach was tied in knots. Not just because so much depended on tonight: it was the thought of meeting Felix himself.

This wasn't a date, she reminded herself.

But it felt weirdly like one.

Worse, she was looking forward to seeing him. Fencing with him. Which she really shouldn't—not when the fairground was depending on her. She had to keep things strictly business. Even if Felix Gisbourne did have an incredibly sensual mouth that made her want to trace it with the tip of her forefinger, before reaching up to kiss him really, really slowly.

Which was utterly ridiculous, and she should know better.

She parked and walked into the hotel reception at five

minutes to seven, remembering Alexis's instructions to do the catwalk strut.

'Mr Gisbourne is expecting me,' she said.

'Miss Bell?'

'Ms,' Daisy corrected with a smile.

'Of course. If you'd like to wait over there, madam?'

Butterflies stampeded in her stomach as she sat down. Did it make her look too keen, being early? On the other hand, she'd failed to turn up for their meeting that morning, so maybe this would redress the balance. Would he make her wait, just to make the point about punctuality, or would he come down straight away?

The doors of the lift slid open and he walked out of the lift. He was wearing a dark grey suit—a slightly different cut, she noticed, so it wasn't the one he'd worn to the fairground—teamed with a pristine white shirt and another understated silk tie. The butterflies in her stomach did a victory roll as he glanced over to her and she saw his jaw drop.

Willing her face to look calm and confident and completely belie how she really felt, she stood up and sashayed towards him.

No way could the pocket Venus in the hotel lobby be Daisy Bell.

Felix had to look twice, and then a third time.

But she strode confidently towards him and he realised that it really was her.

He would never have guessed in a million years that she'd scrub up so well. Her hair was the colour of a new conker, and just as shiny, falling in soft waves to her shoulders; it was a crime to keep it stuffed inside that oversized cap she wore at work. And that shapeless boiler suit had hidden a perfect hourglass shape. Her little black dress was demure and understated, no plunging neckline or clinging skirts, but it showed off her curves to perfection. If she'd worn elbow-length gloves and a big hat, she could've been a ringer for Audrey Hepburn.

Daisy Bell was utterly gorgeous. She was nothing like the women he usually dated, and absolutely nothing like the women that his mother was perpetually lining up for him. But she was pure energy, combined with a quick wit and a sassy mouth wrapped in a body that made all his hormones go straight into party mode.

Felix couldn't remember the last time he'd felt an attraction this strong.

And he *wanted*. So badly that it shocked him to the core.

'No jeans or boiler suits, you said. I trust this passes muster?' she asked coolly.

His comment had clearly stung. Felix unglued his tongue from the roof of his mouth. 'I apologise for that. I wasn't having a go at you.'

'No?'

'Wrong phrase. I meant simply that there was a dress code, and I didn't want you to feel uncomfortable if…' He grimaced. 'I'm digging myself into a bigger hole here.'

'Indeed.'

He sighed. 'Bill warned me you were touchy about sexism and could give as good as you get.'

'Did he, now?' she asked dryly.

He knew it was a rhetorical question, so he didn't bother answering it; instead, he said quietly, 'You look stunning.'

She looked utterly taken aback, and then she blushed. Right to the roots of her hair, giving Felix all kinds of thoughts that he had no intention of giving voice to. And intriguing him, too; it seemed as if she wasn't used to compliments. Strange. Daisy Bell was seriously striking, when she wasn't hiding behind her chief-mechanic clothes. Surely men told her all the time how beautiful she was?

And that look in her eyes, quickly masked, told him that the attraction was mutual—even though he was pretty sure he was nothing like the men she usually dated, either.

There was a definite connection between them.

So what were they going to do about this?

Mixing business and pleasure was a mistake he didn't make. Ever. But Daisy Bell really tempted him to break all his rules. Tempted him to reach out and twirl a strand of her hair round his forefinger, to see if it felt as soft and silky as it looked. To kiss her, to find out if her sea-green eyes turned the colour of jade when she was aroused.

She looked at his mouth, and he knew from her expression that she was thinking exactly the same thing—wondering what it would be like. How he would taste. How electric it would be between them...

He needed to get this back on professional terms, and fast. He held his hand out to her. 'Thank you for coming to meet me tonight, Daisy. Shall we go and eat—and talk business?'

Daisy let Felix take her hand, and it felt as if the blood had started to fizz in her veins. She knew it was the same for him, too, because colour slashed across his cheekbones. He blushed just as he'd made her blush all over with a compliment—one that she'd seen in his eyes was genuine, not just a line he was spinning her.

What on earth was happening? She never, but never, behaved like this.

Part of her wanted to turn tail and run back to the safety of her boiler suit and her workshop. But part of her was intrigued by the possibility that she could reduce this quick, clever man to a puddle of hormones, the same way he affected her. Just supposing…

No. This was business. She couldn't let sex get in the way of the most important thing in her life—saving the fairground. It was too much of a risk.

She took a deep breath and let him lead her through to the dining room. The waiter ushered them to their table, but Felix was the one who held the chair out for her. He had perfect manners as well as a perfect body.

She really shouldn't be thinking about his body.

'Thank you,' she said politely.

He gave her a slight bow. 'Pleasure.'

Every single female in the room was staring at him, but it didn't seem to bother him. Maybe he was used to it. Or maybe he just hadn't noticed.

He glanced at the wine list and asked, 'Would you prefer red or white?'

'Not for me, thanks—I'm driving—but don't feel that you have to go without,' she said politely.

He smiled. 'Water's fine for me. Still or sparkling?'

'Sparkling, please.'

He gave the order to the waiter, and she skimmed down the menu. 'I'm torn between the lamb and the salmon.' Unable to resist the pun, she looked at him over the edge of the menu. 'Do you think they'd let me have a moggie bag?'

He glanced over at the plates of the other diners. 'The portions here aren't that big. But, if you can't manage it, we can ask.'

He'd taken her seriously? She laughed. 'Mr Gisbourne, you're being very slow tonight. Hel-lo—*moggie* bag?'

'Very funny.' He rolled his eyes. 'I didn't pick it up first time round because I'm distracted. Because someone is wearing lapis lazuli right where I'd really, really like to kiss her.'

Suddenly, Daisy was the one who was distracted—imagining it. Felix's mouth was gorgeous, well-shaped, with tiny grooves at each side that told her he laughed a lot. How would it feel, tracing a path across her skin, skimming her collarbone the way her borrowed necklace did?

He'd just said something incredibly suggestive. Outrageous, even. But she didn't think he was the kind of man who made that sort of comment to a woman he'd only just met: instead, she had the distinct feeling that he'd spoken his thoughts aloud without realising it. Felix the businessman might possibly have admitted to being distracted, but he definitely wouldn't have said what was distracting him. That'd be tantamount to handing his business opponent a weapon on a silver platter.

So, instead, she focused on what he'd said before. 'You really think I'm one of these women who nibbles on a lettuce leaf?'

He raised an eyebrow. 'Are you?'

'I plan,' she informed him, 'to order three courses, and petits fours with my coffee, and enjoy every single scrap. What's the point of coming to a restaurant that has a reputation for phenomenal food if you're not going to savour your meal?' She spread her hands. 'I can assure you, the only way I'd eat just a couple of mouthfuls of anything is if we ordered a tasting menu—and then I'd expect quite a few dishes.'

'A woman after my own heart. Good.' He looked approving.

Well, they had some common ground. This was a good thing.

For *business*, she reminded herself.

When the waiter brought their water, Daisy ordered the asparagus soldiers with DIY hollandaise, followed by the salmon and then a trio of puddings.

'So you get a taste of different things?' he asked when he'd given the waiter his own order.

'Absolutely.'

He smiled at her. 'So tell me—how come you have a cat who thinks he's a dog?'

'He was this tiny little kitten who walked into the workshop a couple of years ago and curled up on the engine.'

'Tiny?'

'He was, back then. When I stopped for lunch, he came and sat on my lap. And then he climbed up to my shoulders and miaowed very softly into my ear until I gave him a bit of the salmon from my salad.' She shrugged. 'I put notices in the ticket office and the local shops, and I took him home with me until he was claimed. But nobody claimed him, so I kept him. We called him Titan as a joke, just because he was so tiny—but he grew into his name.'

'And became your guard cat.'

'Absolutely. Shout at me, and you'll have a big ginger cat in front of you with an arched back, his fur completely on end, and some very sharp claws being waved at you. Not to mention the growling.'

Felix laughed. 'He really does think he's a dog, then.'

'A superior dog. But he's good company. I'm glad he adopted me. Do you have pets?'

Felix shook his head. 'My parents have dogs. But I travel a lot, so it wouldn't be fair.'

So he wasn't the kind of man who stayed in one place for long. It was a warning, and she noted it.

Before she could say anything else, the waiter appeared with their first courses.

Felix eyed her plate with interest. 'I can see why you picked that. It's an engineer thing, isn't it?'

She looked at him, surprised. He actually understood? The men she'd dated in the past wouldn't have picked that up. They'd have assumed that she was flirting with them.

Then again, this wasn't a date.

At her nod, he asked, 'So how does it work?'

'You cut the top off the egg, add a little of the butter from the spoon, and a teensy bit of white vinegar from this pipette, then dip the asparagus into the yolk and mix it. Like this.' She demonstrated.

When she licked the sauce from the tip of her asparagus, she glanced across at him—and realised that his pupils had dilated and his mouth was parted slightly.

She hadn't been flirting with him—not intentionally, anyway. But seeing his reaction went straight to her head. This was the man who'd just put an image in her head about him giving her a necklace of kisses. An image she couldn't shift. So maybe he deserved an image in his own head. Time for a little retaliation. She maintained eye contact, dipped the asparagus in the sauce again and took her time licking the sauce from it.

By the time she'd finished eating the first spear, Felix was practically hyperventilating.

'You did that on purpose, didn't you?' he asked.

She pretended to consider the question, then gave him an impish smile. 'Yes. Though, to be fair, you did start it.'

'How?'

'Remember what you said about this?' She indicated her borrowed necklace.

'I said that *out loud*?' He looked horrified. 'I apologise.'

So he hadn't intended to say it. The fact that she'd disturbed his cool enough to make him behave so out of character sent a warm feeling all the way through her.

'No problem.' Honesty compelled her to add, 'And I shouldn't have flirted with you. It isn't fair to your partner.'

'I don't have a partner.' He paused. 'And I wasn't intending to flirt with you, either. It isn't fair to *your* partner.'

She took a deep breath. 'I don't have one, either.' And, just in case he thought that was an offer, she said, 'There's no time—not with work.'

'People don't tend to be very understanding if you put your job before them,' he said, sounding rueful.

Was that why he was single—because he was a workaholic and his ex had given him an ultimatum: the job or her?

She'd had that same ultimatum given to her. With an added twist that still made her angry when she thought about it. 'Tell me about it,' she said, rolling her eyes. She'd just bet that his reaction had been the same as hers: he'd chosen his job. 'And I apologise for teasing you. I suppose it was a case of revenge is hors d'oeuvres.'

His mouth gave that little quirk she found so attractive. 'And I thought it was meant to be sweet.'

'Ah, no. Pudding's something else. I might consider sharing, if I get a taste of your lemon mousse.'

He laughed, those beautiful eyes crinkling at the corners.

When he was relaxed, like this, he seemed more approachable.

Touchable.

She really had to stop thinking like that, because he was off limits.

'I like you, Daisy Bell,' he said. 'I like your style. But I don't think I'm going to be able to look at you until you've finished your asparagus.'

'Try some,' she invited. 'This is fabulous.'

He shook his head. 'I'm fine, thanks. But take my mind off what you just did to me. Tell me how the museum started.'

CHAPTER FOUR

It was a safe subject. No way could she mess this up by flirting with him. Relieved, Daisy began to explain. 'My great-great-grandfather was an engineer in the textile industry, but he could see how steam engines could work with fairground rides. When my great-grandfather—the one who made the gallopers—took over, Bell's were already a household name on the showman circuit.'

'So the museum's based on your family heritage?'

She nodded. 'The demand for rides changed over the years, so my grandfather decided to wind up the business. But my grandmother was from a showman's family and they'd collected some of the machines our family made. Bill took over and added to the collection. You could buy rides really cheaply at one point—sometimes all we had to do was pick up the scrap and haul it to the workshops for restoration—but over the last few years steam engines have become seriously collectable. We could never afford to buy the machines we have now if we had to start again from scratch.'

'Is your father an engineer, too?' Felix asked.

'He designs industrial lifts—well, he did. He's about

to retire. He thinks the fairground is fun, but there's no future in it.' And that she was wasting her talents when she could've made a real name for herself in engineering.

'What about Bill's children?'

Daisy bit her lip. 'Bill and Nancy couldn't have kids. Which is such a shame, as they would've been brilliant parents.'

'I got the impression,' Felix said, 'that Bill thinks of you practically as his daughter.'

She nodded. 'We see things the same way.'

'Are your brothers interested in the fairground?' Felix asked.

She frowned. 'How do you know about my brothers?'

'Bill told me that you're the youngest of four.'

'They're engineers, too, but they see things Dad's way. Ed builds bridges, Ben designs cars, and Mikey works in irrigation systems.' She sighed. 'Being the much-awaited little girl, I was a huge disappointment to my mother. I was never into pink and frilly stuff. If she put me in a dress and told me to play with my dolls, she'd come in ten minutes later to find I'd left them exactly where she'd put them, and I was busy making something with one of my brothers' construction kits or taking something apart to see how it worked.'

'Somehow, I can imagine that,' Felix said with a smile—a smile that said he was on her side.

'Sometimes I wish I'd been the oldest. They all might've found it a bit easier to accept.'

'What, that you wanted to be an engineer, too?'

'Not so much that.' She fiddled with the asparagus.

'What, then?'

'If I'd gone to uni to study engineering, they would've been fine about it.'

Felix looked surprised. 'You don't have a degree?'

'I'm the only one of us who doesn't.' She bit her lip. 'The thing is, I always knew what I wanted to do, and a degree would just have held me back for three years. So I compromised; I stayed at school to do my A levels, then trained as a mechanic.'

'Which I'd guess wasn't an easy option, either. Were there any other girls on the course?'

'I was the only one.' She grimaced. 'It took me until halfway through my course to persuade my tutors and the other students that I was there solely because I wanted to do the job, and not because I was looking for a man.'

She still wasn't. Even if the one sitting opposite her was a particularly fine specimen and had fine laughter-lines at the corners of those stunning grey eyes.

'Ouch,' Felix said. 'So I take it you had to come top in your exams to prove to everyone you were serious?'

'Try every single assignment,' she said dryly.

'And they gave you a hard time?'

She shrugged. 'I qualified, and that's the main thing.' She sighed. 'I know it disappointed my parents and my brothers, but I love what I do. It's who I am.'

'Family expectations, eh?' he said, startling her: she hadn't thought he would understand. But the expression in his eyes, hastily covered, told her he too must have disappointed his family in some way.

'It's the same for you, isn't it?' she asked.

There was a long, long pause, and then he nodded. 'Except I'm the oldest rather than the youngest.'

'So what were you supposed to do?'

'Become the third generation in the family stock-broking business.' He attacked his mushrooms. 'Luckily my sisters did it for me.'

'What's so bad about being a stockbroker?'

That made him lift his head and look her straight in the eye. 'You really have to *ask* that?'

'I'd say you didn't want to do it because it's not your dream.'

'Absolutely. I like fixing things. Like you, I suppose,' he said thoughtfully. 'Except I fix businesses.'

Daisy raised an eyebrow. 'So you admit that you're an asset stripper?'

'No, and if you bother to look me up on the Internet you'll see exactly what I do.'

She spread her hands. 'OK, so that was unfair of me. And I haven't done my homework on you. I meant to.'

'But you got caught up in the engine you were working on this morning?'

She smiled wryly. 'Yes. I've been working on it for a while, and today was my first day back on it. That's why I lost track of time and was late for the meeting.'

He coughed. 'Late?'

'All right, you had to come and find me. And I've already apologised for that.' What else did he want her to do?

An unbidden image floated into her head of apologising to him in a much more personal way. With a kiss.

Oh, no. What on earth was wrong with her? This was meant to be a business conversation. She needed to get things back on track, right now. 'You were going to tell me what's wrong with the way we do things.'

'For a start, you've got all that land and you're not using it.'

'Of course we're using it. It's a play area for children, and pretty gardens for people to stroll in. Everyone loves our gardens.'

'But the land isn't earning you any extra money.'

'So what are you suggesting—that we should sell it to a property developer?'

He frowned. 'Why do you keep thinking the worst of me, Boots?'

She felt her face heat. 'Sorry. It's…'

'A defence mechanism?' he suggested.

'No, I…' Her voice faded. Maybe he was right. Usually she always looked for the good, but she was deliberately trying to see Felix's dark side. It was a defence mechanism, because she found the combination of the way he looked and his quick mind seriously attractive, tempting her to ignore her common sense and break her personal rules. 'Tell me what you were going to say.'

'For a start, the fairground would be a really unusual venue for a wedding.'

Daisy shook her head. 'I did think about that, actually, but when I looked into how much it costs to get a licence for weddings I realised that it wouldn't pay for itself. Besides, we don't have a hall big enough to cater for a reception.'

'You could use a marquee, in summer.'

'Even when it's wet?' She pulled a face. 'Yes, the gondolas would be fabulous for bride-and-groom photographs. But summer weekends are our biggest earners. Holding a wedding reception would mean having to close to the public and lose a day's takings.'

'Not necessarily. You could close in the evenings—that's when the fairground could be exclusive to the wedding party.'

An unobtrusive waiter cleared their empty plates away and brought their main courses through.

'You also need to look at your prices and the number of visitors,' Felix said. 'I assume you do know that?'

She frowned. 'Didn't Bill talk you through that? Yes, of course we do. We have a proper computerised system for tickets, otherwise we'd run into trouble with the tax people. We know exactly how much we take each day. We also know who visits, and whether they're buying individual tickets, or a family ticket, or using a season ticket.'

'Then you need to analyse the stats properly and see if you have the right pricing structure.'

She sighed. 'How do I get it through to you, Felix? We're about heritage, not making huge profits. That's why I want a sponsor, not someone who's going to invest and have a stake in the fairground. I don't want to hike up the admission price and make it too expensive for families to visit. I want people to come back because they've had a great time and they don't feel they've been fleeced.'

'You don't have to hike the prices. But at the moment when they buy their tickets they can have as many rides as they like. Maybe you could look more closely at that,' Felix said. 'Do a deal where you offer so many rides as part of the admission price, but if people want additional rides they pay for them. That way, it's fair usage—the heavier users pay more.'

'I'd rather not put extra pressure on the staff to take money,' Daisy said. 'Besides, if we're handling money in the fairground other than in the ticket office, café or shop, the insurance company will see it as extra risk and our premiums will go sky high—an extra cost we could do without.'

'Not if you do it as a ticket system, or with tokens that don't have monetary value outside the fairground.

Then you won't have to worry about extra cash tills or security.'

She liked the way he thought on his feet. And the way he backed up his arguments.

Again, she met his eyes, and wished she hadn't. Right now they were a cool, analytical grey, and she could just imagine them darkening with desire. The way they had when she'd teased him with her asparagus. And it would be oh, so easy to…

No. The fairground had to come first. She pulled herself together. 'That's definitely worth considering. Thank you. Anything else?'

'Is there a village hall nearby?'

'The nearest one's five miles away.'

'So you could have a community centre. You have the room to build a hall. If you had moveable seating, you could use it for wedding receptions, for shows and a cinema, and any seasonal events, as well as hiring it out to groups—who will then use your café facilities. You could do educational events and children's parties. I see from the website that you already do something special at Hallowe'en and Christmas.'

She nodded. 'We don't have a ghost train—Bell's never built any—but I'd love one. At the moment for Hallowe'en we do a steam-train ride with pumpkin-lanterns lighting the way, and all the staff and volunteers wear fancy dress that evening. At Christmas, Bill's a brilliant Santa. And one of the local farmers has a small herd of reindeer that he brings at weekends.' She smiled. 'We do trips on the steam train to Santa's grotto, and we have fairy lights all along the route. The kids love it.'

'So having a hall would fit in nicely. You could decorate it as Santa's grotto for your Christmas events, hold pantomimes and music-hall evenings there, and maybe get local craftsmen to have stalls at certain times of the year. Plus it would be easier to keep private than a marquee. It'd be a really flexible space.'

'But it's not a short-term solution—and building it would cost.'

'You have to speculate to accumulate.'

'What a cliché.' Was he really not listening to her? 'Besides, to do that, you need money.'

'Not necessarily. That's where external investment comes in,' Felix suggested.

'And external investors want to see a good return on their money. No way would a sponsor agree to build a hall for us, even if we named it after them.' Daisy shook her head. 'You're still missing the point. I keep telling you, it isn't about profit. It's about keeping our heritage alive.'

'If you don't make a profit, how can you afford to maintain the rides?' he asked. 'And, if you want to buy neglected vintage ones that you can restore to working condition, you need an investor, Daisy.'

'A sponsor,' she corrected. 'And you're offering?'

The second the words were out of her mouth she realised that they could be interpreted in a different way. Particularly as she was staring at his beautifully shaped mouth.

She dragged her gaze up slightly, and realised that he was staring at her mouth, too.

Bad.

This was meant to be business.

So why couldn't she get the idea of pleasure out of her head?

'Offering to work with the museum, I mean,' she elaborated—and then was annoyed with her voice for croaking. Oh, no. The last thing she needed was for him to think that she wanted him to offer something much more personal.

Even though part of her did.

'I'm still thinking about it,' Felix said. 'I want to spend a couple of days shadowing Bill and see how everything works.' His gaze held hers a fraction longer than necessary. 'Or shadowing you.'

Absolutely not. Apart from the fact that Felix looked far too pristine to know his way around an engine, spending too much time in his company would be a bad move. The more she talked with him and sparred with him, the more attracted she was to him. And she couldn't afford to be tempted by him. 'You'd be better off systematically shadowing everyone so you get a better idea of how it all fits together,' she said. 'Start with a stint in the coffee bar, do a shift in the shop, then a bit on each ride. And, if you're very good, I might even let you—'

The sudden heat in his eyes made her stop.

'Let me what, Daisy?' he asked, his voice ever so slightly husky. And oh, so sensual. Like melted chocolate.

She hadn't meant the words to come out that way. Hadn't meant to stop mid-sentence. To offer things she shouldn't offer.

What was it about this man that made her unable to think straight?

She pulled herself together with difficulty. 'Drive one of the trains.'

His expression told her that driving a train wasn't the kind of reward he'd had in mind.

Thinking about what he'd consider a fitting reward made her wriggle slightly on the chair.

'Right.' He was looking at her mouth again. As if he wanted to taste it.

The crazy thing was, she wanted him to do it. Despite the fact that they were in a public place and she barely knew him and it would be completely unprofessional of her.

'So why is the fairground so short of money?'

The question came out of left field, and she lifted her chin, scenting a challenge. 'Nobody's embezzling, if that's what you're suggesting. We spent a fair bit last year on rescuing a ride—a chair-o-plane.'

'A what?'

'A roundabout with swing chairs instead of horses. The chairs move out to the side as the roundabout rotates—it's like flying. Maybe it was a bit reckless to use up so much of our reserves, but it was too good an opportunity to miss. And we didn't expect idiots to break in and vandalise the place, or the insurance company to weasel out of paying the claim. Plate glass isn't cheap.'

'Yet the café's fixed. Where did you get the money to do that?'

She looked away. 'That's my business.'

'Daisy?'

She sighed. 'Just don't tell Bill. I said I'd guilt-tripped the insurance company into changing its mind.'

'He'll find out the truth when he looks at the accounts,' Felix warned.

'And by then it'll be too late for him to protest.'

'Where did you get the money?' he asked again, his voice very soft.

'I spoke to the bank and am going to free up some of the equity in my house. *Don't* tell Bill,' she warned again.

'I underestimated you,' Felix said. 'I won't make that mistake again.'

'Good. Because I might be all gussied up right now, but this isn't who I am.'

To her surprise, he reached across the table and squeezed her hand. The pressure of his fingers made heat coil low in her belly.

'I think, right now, you're the one doing the underestimating.'

'Of you?' she asked.

'No. Of yourself.' He released her hand again, but something in his eyes told her that he'd felt the same heat. The same weird connection.

So she resorted to teasing when her pudding arrived, licking her spoon while holding Felix's gaze and enjoying the fact that Felix's colour deepened.

Why had she never understood just how much fun flirting could be?

Maybe she'd been flirting with the wrong men.

'Boots.' His voice had gone all husky, sexy as hell.

'What?'

His mouth had a wicked quirk. 'Open wide.'

She felt colour shooting into her own face.

'I promised you a taste.'

The pudding. He meant the pudding. But her head was already imagining something completely different. Something that definitely wouldn't happen in the middle of a restaurant with two Michelin stars.

He held out a spoonful of his lemon mousse.

Oh, help. She needed to get herself back under control. And fast. Throwing herself at the man who might just invest in their fairground would be such a stupid thing to do. 'Er—it's OK. I'm full,' she fibbed.

'Chicken.'

Her face heated even more. *He knew.*

'You're allowed to change your mind.' He smiled. 'Because I have my eye on your chocolate brownie. Kind of a *quid pro quo.*'

'You want a taste?'

'Oh, yes,' he drawled. 'I want a taste.'

She still had completely different thoughts in her head. Thoughts that she suspected he shared, given his expression as he ate the spoonful of chocolate brownie she offered him.

Oh, this was bad.

They'd just eaten in the best restaurant for miles.

And, apart from the pudding, she hadn't paid a scrap of attention to the food; she'd been so focused on Felix. Talking to him about the fairground. Finding out more about him—though he'd managed to change the subject fairly quickly on that score.

She ordered a double espresso when the waiter returned, really needing the jolt of caffeine. She felt as if she'd been drinking champagne rather than sparkling water—or maybe Felix had gone to her head. When they reached for the petits fours at the same time and their fingers brushed, it was like the electric sparks at the top of the dodgems.

She'd never met anyone who had this kind of effect on her before.

'I've enjoyed this evening,' he said softly when she'd finished her coffee.

'Me, too,' she admitted. 'But I'd better get back.'

'For Titan?'

He remembered her cat's name?

Well, of course he would. Felix Gisbourne was the kind of man who paid attention to things. It didn't mean anything else. 'Yes. So do you mind if we get the bill?'

He shrugged. 'No need. It's my bill.'

'Absolutely not. This was a business discussion. So it's a fifty-fifty split.'

'And,' he said softly, 'it was also pleasure. I enjoyed having dinner with you, Boots. So I'm paying.' At her narrowed eyes, he added, 'Don't argue.'

She shook her head.

'Tell you what. If you're that unhappy, you can feed me tomorrow night.'

He wanted to see her again?

'Work or...?' She hesitated to say the word 'pleasure'.

He said it for her. 'I've enjoyed your company tonight.' He leaned forward, dropping his voice so that only she could hear it. 'Not to mention the fact that you're the most interesting woman I've met in years.'

Interesting. Intellectual, then, not sexy and gorgeous. Well, who had she been trying to kid? Even Alexis couldn't make her into a goddess. The material just wasn't there.

'You engage my head as well as my libido,' he said. 'And that's rare.'

She dragged in a breath. He could've been talking for her—obviously with the gender reversed.

She wasn't looking for a relationship of any description. She liked her life just fine as it was. And he'd told her that he was a workaholic who didn't stay in one place too long. Having a fling with him would be complete and utter insanity.

And yet...

'All right,' she said. 'I'll feed you tomorrow night.'

He smiled. 'I'll look forward to it.'

He came round to her side of the table to help her out of the chair. His manners were as impeccable as his dress sense, she thought. 'I'll walk you to your car.'

They walked in silence out of the hotel. With each step her heart beat faster, harder.

Was Felix going to kiss her in the late-spring moonlight?

Did she want him to?

When they reached the car, he whistled. 'Now, that's *nice*.'

'And it's not mine,' she admitted. 'It belongs to Ben, my brother—his dream car.'

'And yours?'

'E-type Jaguar. Red. You?'

'Aston Martin DB5. Silver.'

She burst out laughing. 'The name's Bond. Felix Bond.'

'The name's Gisbourne,' he corrected huskily. 'Felix Gisbourne.'

And then he dipped his head and brushed his mouth against hers. So sweet. So light. Offering and promising at the same time.

He did it again, and this time she found herself responding, opening her mouth below his and letting him deepen the kiss. And the next thing she knew, her arms were round his neck and his arm was wrapped around her with his hand splayed against her spine, pulling her so close that she could feel his arousal hard against her belly. She couldn't even remember the last time someone had kissed her like this, or when she just hadn't been able to get enough of someone's kiss; it felt as if she were riding on a waltzer, whirling round, with the lights flashing and the music playing.

When he finally broke the kiss and took a single step back from her, she felt lost.

'*À demain*, Boots,' he said softly.

Daisy was completely lost for words. She couldn't think of a single smart retort. Instead, she touched a hand to her mouth in wonder and climbed into the car.

Hell.

She couldn't remember how to drive.

He'd fried her brain with that kiss.

He knocked on the glass and she wound the window down.

'Daisy? Are you all right?'

No. 'You kissed me,' she whispered.

'You kissed me back.'

She gripped the steering wheel to stop her hands shaking. 'Felix, this isn't a good idea.'

'I know.' His eyes were intense, so dark they were almost black. 'But there's something about you that makes me want to do all kinds of things I know aren't sensible.'

'That makes two of us.'

Oh, no. She really hadn't meant to say that aloud.

'I'm going, Boots. Before I give in to temptation and haul you out of that car and over my shoulder and back to somewhere much more private.' He brushed her cheek with the back of his fingers. 'See you tomorrow. Sweet dreams.'

Her dreams definitely weren't going to be sweet. They were going to be X-rated.

She had no idea how she managed to drive home. But then she was in the safety of her little terraced cottage, with Titan curled on her lap.

'He's dangerous,' she told the cat. 'I should stay out of his way.'

Though she knew full well she wouldn't.

CHAPTER FIVE

THE next morning, Daisy washed her borrowed dress and hung it to dry in her back garden, ready for ironing and returning to Alexis that evening. Then she cycled to work the way she usually did, with Titan sitting in the wicker basket at the front.

To her surprise, Felix was waiting for her outside the workshop.

'Daisy, Daisy…on a bicycle built for two?' he teased.

'Very funny.' But she still liked the fact he could sing one of the lines. And that he'd got the words right.

'I didn't realise the song was actually called "Daisy Bell". Were you named after it?'

She climbed off the bicycle, waited for Titan to leap out of the basket and propped her bike against the wall inside the workshop. 'No. I was named after my grandmother. Who was also Daisy Bell, after she married my grandfather.'

'I see. By the way, I brought you a moggie bag.' He waved it in front of her. 'You said that someone's partial to salmon.' Titan miaowed, as if in full agreement. 'So I went to sweet-talk the chef.'

'You're trying to bribe my cat?' she asked as she opened the workshop door.

'To get in your good books?' He laughed. 'Maybe. You look good in those jeans, Boots.'

The compliment made her want to beam at him, but she didn't want him to think she was needy. So she simply shrugged. 'They're sensible clothes for working here. Unlike,' she added pointedly, 'Your suit, which will get really grubby if you hang around the steam engines.'

'You don't actually own a dress, do you?'

'Did you not notice what I was wearing last night?' she countered.

He moved closer. 'I noticed, all right. Did you not notice what effect you had on me? I don't usually kiss strange women in car parks.'

He thought she was strange?

That hurt. She was used to that reaction and usually let it wash over her—but from Felix, particularly as he'd been the one to initiate that kiss, it stung. As if he'd pushed her into the middle of a nettle patch. 'Whatever, Mr Gisbourne,' she drawled.

'Let me clarify that—I meant strange as in someone I don't know very well, not strange as in weird.'

Had her thoughts shown on her face, or was he just really good at reading body language? Either way, it wasn't good for her peace of mind.

'And I think you don't own a skirt or a dress. I think you borrowed more than just your brother's car.'

He had her pegged, all right. She took refuge in sassiness. 'What, you think my brother's a cross-dresser?'

'No. I think your brother's married with two little boys who love coming to see their Aunty Daisy because she takes them on the gallopers and lets them ride with the driver of the steam train instead of in the carriage with everyone else. So an educated guess would say that you borrowed the dress from your sister-in-law. Who, before she married, was a very talented make-up artist, and who sometimes does charity makeovers to raise money for her favourite sister-in-law's fairground.'

'You've been talking to Bill.'

'I've been talking to Maureen in the ticket office,' he corrected. 'And I'm meant to be getting her a mug of tea. Except I was on a mission with a moggie bag.' He dipped his head and kissed the corner of her mouth, sweet and full of promise. 'I'll see you later, Boots.'

He scratched the cat behind his ears. 'Don't scoff all the salmon at once,' he instructed, and handed Daisy the bag before sauntering off with a wide, wide smile.

How did he do that? How could just a couple of words, a teasing grin and that tiny, tiny touch of his mouth against hers send her into such a flat spin?

Felix spent the day diligently shadowing Maureen in the ticket office and Shelley in the café, being charming to the visitors, but his head was full of Daisy.

She intrigued him. He'd never met anyone like her: a woman who spent her days in a boiler suit and purple Doc Martens with flowers on them, and yet in a simple black dress and with her hair loose she looked like Venus. A woman who needed to know how things worked, who could take things apart and fix them; a woman so fiercely loyal to her family and who believed in her job to the point where she'd make sacrifices for them without a second thought—she'd taken out a loan to fix the café windows, knowing she'd never see her money back again.

Daisy Bell had layers. Layers he wanted to unpeel.

But, even more than that, he wanted to kiss her again. The way her mouth had opened under his, the way she'd held him while he'd explored her mouth—even the memory of it put him in serious need of a cold shower. He hadn't been this attracted to anyone in years, and it threw him.

This was meant to be a business opportunity that was different enough to keep his interest and even be challenging. Seducing the deputy manager-cum-chief mechanic would be a seriously bad idea. But there was something about her.

Something he couldn't resist.

He managed to keep his distance from her for most of the day, but by mid-afternoon his resolve had weakened to the point where he offered to do the tea round. And Daisy happened to be the last one on his list.

He could hear her singing as he reached the workshop door; today's songs were from *Oklahoma*. Remembering what Bill had said about knowing that something was wrong when Daisy didn't sing, he smiled. He hadn't put her off her stride too much last night, then.

Titan was curled up on the top of the engine. He opened one eye and stared at Felix.

'Visitors,' Felix said hopefully.

The cat didn't move.

'What, you want more salmon? That's greedy.'

The cat continued to treat him to a steady, unblinking gaze.

'You're a shark in a fur coat.'

It was surreal, talking to a cat. Crazy.

'All right. I'll bring you another moggie bag to-

morrow. Tell her she's got visitors. And it's time for tea.'
He lifted the mug.

The cat jumped down; a couple of seconds later,
there was an 'Ow!' and Daisy emerged from under the
steam engine.

'Oh. It's you,' she said.

The words were all casual. So was the tone.

But her eyes were giving him a completely different message.

'Yup, it's me.' Her boiler suit was still shapeless and
covered in oil. Her hair was hidden by the baseball cap.
There were smudges of oil on her face. Yet she still
made his blood heat.

'What do you want?'

Her expression was wary, so he bit back the word that
rose to his lips. *You.* 'Shelley sent me over with a mug
of tea. It's time for your break.'

'Thank you.'

'Apparently it's your special mug.' Marked 'DB:
Chief Mechanic', with a picture of a steam engine
underneath it. He'd just bet that someone at the fairground had had it specially made for her as a present
for her birthday or Christmas. He'd quickly learned how
much the staff at the fairground adored her; they'd all
told him how she pitched in and helped, no matter what
the situation.

He'd seriously misjudged her when he'd thought she
didn't pull her weight. She did much, much more than that
around here. Daisy Bell was the heart of the fairground.

'About dinner tonight,' he said. 'You promised to
feed me.'

The wary expression grew more pronounced, and
Felix knew he should back off. But the words that came

out of his mouth were the complete opposite of what he'd intended. 'Or are you chickening out?'

She lifted her chin. 'I'm not a coward.'

'Of course you're not. And I'm not a mind reader,' he said. 'So it would be quite helpful if you'd tell me what the arrangements are.'

'What I have in mind,' she said, 'isn't really a "posh suit" type of place.'

He knew immediately that she was paying him back for his comments about her own clothes. Fair enough. He'd been rude to her. And he had the feeling that someone else had said the same kind of thing, had hurt her. Judged her by conventional standards and found her wanting.

Maybe that was why she dressed in shapeless clothes at work: not just for comfort, but to make the point that she was her own woman and she didn't give a damn what people thought. Even though he had a suspicion that, deep inside, it *did* matter to her. 'What do you suggest?' he asked.

'Jeans.' She gave him a level look. 'If you possess any.'

He didn't. But hopefully he had enough time to do something about it. 'Where and when do I meet you?'

'I need to drop my brother's car back to him first— so outside the gates here at quarter to seven.'

He still had no idea what she had planned, but he had a feeling that he was going to enjoy it. 'Quarter to seven it is.'

He needed to find some jeans. He headed back to the café to explain to Shelley that something had come up and he'd do another stint to help tomorrow, had a quick word with Bill, and then drove to the nearest large town. Half an hour later, he'd purchased a pair of faded blue

jeans and a pair of casual suede boots that he guessed
would meet with Daisy's approval. And, given that he
thought she'd object to the kind of shirts he usually
wore with a suit, he also bought a black cashmere
sweater.

When he met her outside the gates to the fairground
at precisely quarter to seven, the look on her face told
him that he'd got it perfectly right.

She looked fabulous, in soft faded denims, a
lavender-coloured sweater, and her glorious hair down.
She'd clearly washed it that evening because it was still
slightly damp and he could smell the strawberry scent
of her shampoo. It made him want to wrap his arms
round her and bury his face in her hair; to stave off
temptation, he shoved his hands in his pockets.

'No Titan?' he asked, nodding to the wicker basket
on the front of her bike.

'Not tonight.' She gestured to the picnic blanket on
the top. 'No room.'

'So where are we going? Do you want to put your
bike in the back of my car?'

She smiled. 'No. We're already here.'

'We're having dinner here?'

'Yup. Tonight, Mr Gisbourne, I'm going to show you
why I love this place so much. Go and park by the ticket
office.' She undid the gate, waited for him to drive
through, then padlocked it shut behind them and cycled
over to meet him. She propped her bike on its stand next
to his car, then took the blanket from her basket as well
as a small cool box.

'Can I carry any of that?' he asked.

'No, you're fine.'

She led him over to the gondola, where she left the

cool box and blanket in the shade, then took him over to the dodgems. 'We'll start here. Choose your car while I sort out the mechanics.' A few moments later, she had the lights on and the music blasting out. 'No bumping,' she warned, when she came back to join him. 'The idea is to dodge each other.'

'And if you crash it damages the cars?' he guessed.

'They're pretty robust, but they're original and I'd rather not take any risks.' She slid behind the wheel of the car next to him and gave him the cheekiest grin he'd ever seen. 'Catch me if you can, Felix.'

It was huge fun, Felix discovered, having the ride to themselves. Daisy's car weaved around the circuit; she'd clearly had a lot of practice because she was really, really good at it. Every time he thought he'd caught her, she spun round and headed in the opposite direction.

But eventually she drew her car to a halt and climbed out. 'Obviously you didn't have a misspent youth.'

No. His parents had never taken him to fairgrounds when he was small, and by his teens he'd wondered what all the fuss was about. Loud music, flashing lights and junk food: it hadn't been his style. Not that he was going to tell her any of that. Instead, he changed the subject. 'I was expecting to hear Elvis, considering you told me this was a 1950s ride.'

She laughed. 'We have Elvis. But most of the time we play music from the early 1960s. Bobby Vee, the Everly Brothers—stuff from my mum's teenage years. The grandparents just love it when they come here. I see them watching their grandchildren, and they're singing their heads off.' She smiled. 'I can remember Granny Bell singing this stuff, too.' She sang a couple of bars of 'Take Good Care of My Baby'.

'So you get your singing talent from your grandmother?' he asked.

'Granny Bell was a showman's daughter. So she could sing, dance, juggle—and she used to tease the boys that she did fire-eating when she was young.'

'Did she?'

'Knowing Granny Bell, probably.' She laughed. 'But she never did anything dangerous with us—much to the boys' disappointment and Mum's relief. We always loved going to see her. She taught us all to juggle.' Her smile broadened. 'With eggs.'

'Hard-boiled?'

'Nope. So we soon learned not to drop them. I juggle with eggs when I do talks at schools. The kids love it as much as the boys and I used to.'

'Sounds like an idyllic childhood.'

'It was.' Unexpectedly, she covered his hand with hers. 'I take it yours wasn't?'

No. Not that he'd intended to let anyone else know how he felt, so how had she guessed? He shrugged. 'It was OK.' He wasn't going to dwell on how much he'd loathed boarding school. Or how often as a child he'd wished his parents would listen to him and let him go to the local day school instead, the way his sisters had. It was old stuff, and he was over it. He just intended to make sure his life was what he wanted it to be now.

'I know how lucky I am,' she said softly. 'My parents were pretty upset when I left school after my A levels, but I think they realised that being stuck in a classroom wasn't for me. And Granny Bell helped. She told them that some people have to do things rather than listen or watch, and I'm one of them. And they saw it, too, and supported me after that.'

'You were close to your grandmother?'

She nodded. 'I still miss her. She died five years ago, and the church was standing-room only at her funeral. Everyone loved Granny Bell.' She shook herself. 'Anyway. Let's go on the gallopers.'

She made sure that all the machinery was switched off on the dodgems, then took him over to the gallopers.

'I converted all the steam engines on the rides to electric, simply because it saves a lot of grief with the health and safety mandarins,' she said.

Lights flickered on all over the roundabout, reflected in the strategically placed mirrors. Even though the evening was quite bright, having the lights on still made the ride look amazing. Felix was beginning to see why Daisy loved the odd mixture of showiness and innocence that was the fairground.

'Choose your horse. Any horse,' she said with a smile, and went into the centre to set up the organ.

Felix had half-expected her to send him round on his own, but she jumped on to the revolving platform and walked round to him, climbing onto the ostrich next to his horse when it was at its lowest.

'Daisy, that's—'

'Something I've done for at least fifteen years, so stop panicking,' she said, reaching across to pat his hand. 'It's not dangerous, because I know what I'm doing, I know where to put my feet and I don't take stupid risks.'

He stopped protesting and just enjoyed the ride. But what he enjoyed more was the sheer pleasure in her face as she sat next to him, one hand resting lightly against the gilded barley-sugar pole.

He couldn't help wondering: what would those clever, capable hands feel like against his skin?

Halfway through the next song, she vaulted lightly off the ostrich and was back at the controls in the centre of the ride, slowing it down as the music came to a halt.

'Enough, or do you want another go?'

'Enough,' he said with a smile. 'You really love this, don't you?'

She patted one of the horses. 'Yes. Do you get it now?'

'If I say no, does that mean I get to try out the other rides?'

She laughed. 'You're on.' She took him over to the swing boats and moved a set of ladders next to one of the boats. 'In you get.'

'Ladies first.'

'So you can stare at my behind? I think not. Anyway, I'm lighter than you. It's best if the heaviest one gets in first.'

'So you can stare at *my* behind?' he retorted.

'All right, all right. Since you're fishing, Mr Gisbourne, you look fabulous in those jeans. Satisfied?'

'It'll do for now.' He climbed up the ladder and stepped into the boat. 'So how old are these?'

'This set was built in the 1920s, though they've been around for a lot longer than that.' She took one of the ropes. 'The harder you pull, the higher it goes.'

It took him a couple of goes before he got the rhythm right, and then it felt incredible. Incredible to be working as a team with Daisy. He was pretty sure that she felt it, too; he could see a mixture of surprise and pleasure in her eyes.

'You have to imagine this with lights and music,' she said as they both stopped pulling and let the swing settle.

'And all around you've got people laughing, forgetting their troubles. That's what the travelling showmen brought to village fairs—sheer entertainment, something to look forward to after months of working hard and trying to make ends meet.'

And the ironic thing was that she, Bill and the fairground staff were trying to do the modern version of it—except they were the ones struggling to make ends meet.

Next, she made him climb the stairs to the top of the helter-skelter, and handed him a rush mat. 'Keep hold of the mat,' she said, 'and don't try to grab on to the sides or you'll burn your hands.'

'Yes, ma'am.'

The ride was much faster than he'd imagined, much more fun. Though there was one thing missing… On his third time round, Felix waited for Daisy at the bottom, helped her to her feet, then bent his head and kissed her.

'What brought that on?' she asked.

She was aiming for cool and calm, he knew, but he could hear the breathiness in her tone. That kiss had affected her as much as it had him, even though it had been light rather than a full-on kiss. 'Isn't that the idea? Kiss me quick, squeeze me slowly?'

'That,' she said, 'is a seaside slogan. We're five miles from the sea.'

He stole another kiss. 'That one was for luck,' he said, smiling at her. 'Which I think is a valid slogan anywhere.'

'Indeed.'

But she was blushing. And she looked incredibly pretty. She didn't need make-up or designer clothes to make her look good. She was perfect just as she was. Felix had to jam his hands back into his pockets to stop himself grabbing her and kissing her properly.

She took him round all the rides, one by one. Then, finally, she took him over to the gondola. 'Remember, when this was in vogue most of the passengers had barely seen a car, much less ridden on one. This one's a bit on the slow side, but that's because there aren't any seatbelts. I have to comply with health and safety legislation, and this is the compromise they agreed.' She smiled. 'It's still a great ride, though. And it was mind-blowing when it first came out.'

'Are you coming in the car with me?' he asked when she walked into the centre to start the engine.

She shook her head. 'I converted this to an electric motor, but I can't walk about on this like I do on the platform of the gallopers.' She smiled wryly. 'I wish now I'd sorted this out on remote control, but never mind. Enjoy.'

The lights were on and the fairground organ was playing, and Felix found himself craning over the side, looking for Daisy and waving to her when he passed her.

When the ride slowed and finally came to a halt, she left the organ playing.

'So what do you think?'

'I enjoyed it. Though I did wonder if I was going to fall out when I went up the hills backwards and seemed to be going forward at a crazy angle.'

She laughed. 'That's the point. I have to admit, this is my favourite out of all of them.' She stroked the carved and gilded side of the gondola car. 'My great-grandfather built this ride. My grandmother worked on it. My uncle rescued it. And I grew up with it. There's a photograph of me riding on this when I was about eighteen months old, sitting next to Dad, smiling my face off. And now the next generation's here: the twins love this one, too.'

Felix could see now that the fairground was her passion; whenever she talked about it, there was that extra sparkle in her eyes. He couldn't help wondering what it would be like if she were to redirect that passion on him. The kisses they'd shared so far had been fairly chaste affairs, but Daisy Bell was definitely a passionate woman; it showed in the curve of her generous mouth.

She spread out the rug, sat down and patted the rug beside her. 'Come on. I promised to feed you.'

Felix discovered that the cool box contained crusty French bread, a creamy Brie, sliced tomatoes and rocket.

'It doesn't have to be a hot meal to be balanced,' she said, opening a tub of hummus and a container full of crudités. 'Notice—vegetables, protein and carbs. Sorry, I'm not quite up to Michelin-star standard.'

'This is lovely,' Felix said, meaning it. He couldn't remember the last time he'd had a picnic with anyone. Or when he'd wanted to lie on his back, looking up at the sky as the sun set.

They finished their meal with ripe nectarines that made a tiny rivulet of juice dribble at the corner of her mouth, and seriously tempted him to lick it off, and finally rich, chocolate brownies. 'I thought I'd better bring these, seeing as you're such a cake fiend,' she teased.

'They're fabulous. Did you make them?'

'No. I can't believe you did a stint in the café and didn't spot Shelley's famous brownies.' She scoffed. 'Talk about unobservant. You're slipping, Mr Gisbourne.'

'I was on the cash desk,' he defended himself. And then he frowned. 'Does Shelley know why you wanted these?'

'Yes. For dinner.' She smiled. 'I often buy something from the café for dinner, because I'm too busy to cook—

or too lazy, depending on how you see it—so don't worry. People aren't going to be gossiping about us.'

'Good.' Finally, he let himself give into temptation, leaned forward and kissed her. 'You taste of nectarines and chocolate.'

'So do you.' She stroked his arm. 'And this is really gorgeous.'

Him, or his sweater?

'So soft.'

The sweater, then.

But it wasn't as soft as her hair. 'So's this. And I really, really need to do this, Daisy.' He slid his hands into her hair. 'This is so lush. Like your mouth. It makes me want to…' He kissed her again.

As the kiss deepened, he lay back against the rug, drawing her down on top of him.

He could feel the softness of her breasts against his chest. He stroked one hand over the lush curve of her bottom and settled the other against the flat of her spine, just as he'd wanted to do all day.

Right here, right now, it was just the two of them. It could've been blowing a gale and hailing and he wouldn't have noticed. His senses were completely filled with Daisy Bell: with her glossy brown hair that smelled of strawberries, her lush mouth that tasted of nectarines, and the softness to her body that made him want to sink into her and lose himself completely.

Best of all, she was kissing him back.

Clearly he'd died and gone to heaven.

But, when he finally surfaced from the kiss, he saw wariness in her face.

'I'm not going to hurt you, Daisy,' he said softly.

'Good.'

He sat up so she was kneeling astride him and cradled on his lap, and wrapped his arms round her. 'I wasn't expecting this to happen, either. But we're going to have to deal with it.'

'We'll be sensible about it,' Daisy said.

'Will we? I can't get you out of my head, Boots. And I have a feeling this whole thing has thrown you as much as it has me.'

'Yes,' she admitted.

'So maybe we should…' Looking into her face was a bad idea. Because her mouth was just centimetres from his. All he had to do was lean forward slightly, and…

'Felix, we can't. This is meant to be business.'

Her eyes were wide and full of panic. Time to back off. He kissed the tip of her nose and released her. 'We're adults. I think we're both capable of separating business and whatever else this thing is, but I'm not going to push you. I'll help you pack up.'

Once he'd shaken the grass off the rug and folded it up and everything was back in the picnic basket, he walked back to where they'd left her bicycle and his car. 'Do you want to put that in the back of my car and I'll drive you home?' he suggested.

She shook her head. 'It's fine. I'll see you tomorrow.'

He smiled at her. 'Thank you for this evening. I enjoyed it. And you're right, I get it, now. It's the lights and the music and the movement. It makes it feel as if the very air is sparkling.'

She blinked at him, looking surprised. 'That's exactly how I feel about it.'

But not all of it's the fairground, Felix thought. A lot of the sparkle's to do with you. And it scares the hell out of me at the same time as making me want more. 'See

you tomorrow, Boots.' He waited until she'd relocked the
gate before driving in the opposite direction towards the
hotel.

Tomorrow suddenly seemed much too far away.

CHAPTER SIX

THE next morning, Felix volunteered to do the tea run. Somehow Daisy ended up being last on his list.

Who was he trying to kid? Of course she was. He'd planned it that way so he could linger a little. Talk to her. Spend time with her.

And right now she was singing, 'Getting To Know You'.

Very appropriate.

Titan opened one eye from his prime position on the engine and stared at him.

'Hey. She has a beautiful voice. Of course I want to listen,' Felix said.

The cat continued to stare, though this time his gaze seemed to be on the brown-paper bag Felix was holding.

'It's your choice, cat. I can't give you any salmon unless I've cleared it with her first,' Felix said. 'So it's in your best interests to tell her she's got a visitor.'

If cats could roll their eyes, he thought, Titan was definitely rolling his. But the cat duly jumped off the engine to fetch Daisy.

Daisy emerged from the other side. 'How long have you been there?' she asked as soon as she saw him.

'Long enough.'

She blushed; right at that moment, shapeless clothes and all, she looked adorable. 'You look like one of the urchins in *Oliver*,' he said.

She laughed, and sang the first few bars of 'Consider Yourself'.

He laughed back. 'I brought you tea and a moggie bag.'

'What, salmon again?' She stroked the cat. 'I know someone who's going to be impossible next week.'

Did she mean when he'd left?

'But thank you. For the tea *and* the salmon.'

Titan miaowed, as if in full agreement.

'So who are you shadowing today?' she asked.

'I was thinking about spending an hour on each of the main rides. Even though I know how they work, it'll help me see your visitor throughput and which ones are the most popular.'

'Want to drive the train?'

When he didn't respond, she looked puzzled. 'Most people leap at the offer. I thought all men wanted to be train drivers when they were little.'

'No. I didn't really travel by train.' He'd always been driven back to boarding school. And not always by his parents; they'd been too busy.

At the time, he'd accepted it at face value, though for a while now the doubts had crowded into his head. Maybe Tabitha had had a point—maybe he hadn't been interesting enough for them, either.

He'd questioned an awful lot of things since the moment three years ago when he'd overheard Tabitha talking to her friends on the balcony of their flat, telling them how she really felt about him. He'd looked at his childhood with a fresh view and he'd wondered if he'd misread it as badly as he'd misread his fiancée. And then he'd hated himself for doubting his family, for letting her make him so paranoid, insecure and needy.

He pushed the thoughts away. *Not now.* He was over Tabitha. He'd moved on. And he didn't intend to let anyone close enough to him again that it would matter if their main concern was his money. His relationships had sharply defined limits nowadays, and they didn't involve his heart. Ever.

'So you've never been on a steam engine?' Daisy asked.

'No.'

'What, not ever?'

He shrugged. 'It's not a big deal.'

'Says you. We'll be steamed up at ten. Meet me at platform one at five to—because you're going to be driving the train.' She wrinkled her nose. 'Mind you, your shirt might get a bit grubby from the smuts.'

He couldn't resist teasing her. 'I could always take it off. Drive bare-chested.'

Colour shot into her face. 'Go and see Maureen. She'll get Mac to lend you one of his boiler suits.'

'Mac being the guy who usually drives the train? Won't he have something to say about me driving it— especially as I've never driven a steam train before?'

'No.' She smiled. 'You'll be with me.'

That said it all. And it was exactly where he wanted to be, right then. With her. Just the two of them. It was completely crazy, and he should know better. But for the life of him he couldn't say no. 'I'll see you later, then.'

Felix met Daisy at the platform at exactly five to ten, dressed in a boiler suit that just about fitted. She'd changed into a clean boiler suit; her hair was still hidden under a cap, but this one was clean and was emblazoned with the word 'Fireman'.

She smiled at him. 'Well, Mr Gisbourne, don't you look fabulous in green?'

'What's the fireman thing about?' he asked.

'You need two people to drive a steam train. You're the driver—you use the steam to move the train. And I'm the fireman; I know the layout of the track, so I know when you're going to need the steam to power the train, and it's my job to make sure it's there for you.'

She produced a red cap with a black band above the visor that said 'Engine Driver'; he recognised it as part of the stock in the shop. 'Pressie for you.'

She really expected him to wear that?

It seemed so.

But any latent grumpiness evaporated when she ushered him on to the train and all the children started waving at him.

'You have to wave back,' she said *sotto voce*. And completely unnecessarily, as he was already doing it. 'Mac's just getting the last of the passengers on board now.'

'So what do all these levers do?' he asked.

She talked him through the levers and valves, pointing out the water gauge. 'That's the most important glass on the train. If the water level's too low, you'll end up with a boiler explosion and you'll wipe out the whole fairground.'

'And you still think it's safe for me to drive?'

She grinned. 'You've got the chief mechanic with you—who's been hanging around this part of a steam train for twenty-odd years, I might add. So what do you think?'

'OK. And what's this can for?'

'Ah, that. It's Mac's tea-billy. Because it lives above

the firehole door, it means the tea's always hot.' She grimaced. 'But Mac's tea is so strong it'd dissolve a spoon, so if he offers you any…'

'Say no?' he asked, laughing back.

'If you value your teeth, yes.' She laughed. 'OK, now blow the whistle—you need two short blasts to signal we're about to move.' She took his hand and placed it on the cable, and desire trickled all the way down his spine. Instead of driving the train, he wanted to tangle his fingers with hers and draw her body close to his. And kiss her.

'Pay attention, Mr Gisbourne. Two blasts.'

He dragged his mind back from fantasyland and pulled the cable twice.

'Release the brake,' she directed. 'That's great. Open the throttle, then shove it most of the way back. Now open it gradually until I tell you to stop.'

And then they were off. The engine juddered, smoke swirled from the chimney and made the air smell sharply of cinders and the steam chuffed. Felix had never experienced anything like it in his life. But suddenly he could see why Daisy was so enthusiastic about it. And, from what he could see, the people lining the route were enjoying the spectacle as much as the passengers were enjoying their trip.

Living heritage. That was what made Daisy tick.

And now he understood exactly why.

'Did you enjoy it?' she asked at the end.

'I loved it,' he answered honestly.

'Good. Because now you're going to help me turn the engine round, ready for Mac to take it out again. And it's a manual turntable.'

'You're telling me we're moving this train *manually*?'

'Just the engine. All eight and a half tonnes of her.

Here, let me do this bit. We need to be a bit precise about where we stop and it's not fair to put that burden on a rookie driver.'

She really played to the crowds, telling them she needed their help to turn the engine. 'After a count of three, I want you to blow.' She jumped out and sorted the rails, saying under her breath so that only Felix could hear her, 'Push the engine anti-clockwise.'

All the children crowded by the fence did exactly what she said, clapping madly as Felix walked the engine round the turntable. She was a real showman, he thought. It was in her blood.

'And now, everyone, we need three cheers for Felix the Driver.'

They were cheering him?

This was surreal. He usually spent his day behind a desk, or looking over businesses he was thinking about working with. This impromptu lesson in driving a steam train and turning an engine round was so far out of his normal world he couldn't begin to compare them. Physically, it was hard work. But it was also enormous fun.

When, he wondered, had his life stopped being fun?

Because now he realised that it had. Daisy had shown him what he was missing. Something he'd been missing for too many years. Again, Tabitha's words came back to him. *Of course I don't love Felix... He's so* dull*!*

He pushed the thought away. He didn't love Tabitha any more. His feelings for her had died the instant he'd discovered why she was really getting married to him. It was the self-doubt he was finding harder to come to terms with; unlike Daisy, he didn't trust himself to see the good in people any more. Not where relationships were concerned. Which was one of the reasons why he'd buried himself in work.

Mac was there to couple the train back to the carriages and take control of the driving again, Rodney took over as the fireman and Felix fell into step beside Daisy as she headed back to her work.

'That was amazing,' he said when they were back in the workshop. 'I think you just gave me something missing from my childhood.' Though he regretted the admission as soon as he saw her eyes darken.

'Felix, you're breaking my heart for the little boy you were. You were lonely, weren't you?'

'Of course I wasn't,' he fibbed. He really hadn't intended to tell her that. Or to let her this close to him. Dangerously close. 'I have two sisters. How on earth could I have been lonely?'

She raised an eyebrow.

'If you tell anyone, I may have to denounce you as a madwoman,' he drawled, affecting disdain.

To his surprise, she stepped forward, slid her arms round him and held him close, as if she really cared how he felt.

As if she wanted to make it better.

Something inside him felt as if it was cracking.

'I won't tell anyone,' she said softly. 'I was lucky; I grew up knowing my whole family loves me—even if they don't approve of my career choice and they drive me crazy by constantly reminding me that I'm the baby of the family.'

'My family loves me,' he protested.

'On their terms? I bet they're still trying to get you into the stockbroking stuff. Especially as you're so good at fixing things.'

She was too close to the truth for his comfort. He needed to distract her, and fast. But the completely wrong thing came out of his mouth. 'Have dinner with me tonight?'

'What, so I have to wear a dress again?'

'Not if we have dinner on my balcony.'

He had to be completely mad. He wasn't in the market for a relationship, and he really ought to put some distance between them, so why was he suggesting seeing her tonight? Why was he suggesting a much more private venue than the hotel dining room?

She released him and took a step back, looking at him through narrowed eyes. 'Your balcony. Which is just off your bedroom, right?'

Strangely enough, her wariness reassured him. 'There aren't any strings, Daisy. Dinner means *dinner.*'

She didn't say a word; her expression said it all for her: *does it?*

And that gave him the courage to say the weird, conflicting feelings in his head out loud. 'I admit, I find you attractive—and I think it's mutual—but I'm asking you to eat with me tonight because I enjoy your company, not because I'm planning to take you to bed.' Even though he'd like to do that, too. 'I'll send a taxi for you, because I'd like to share a couple of glasses of wine with you.'

She moistened her lower lip, and it was all he could do to stop himself dipping his head and kissing her. What was it about this woman that turned his common sense upside down?

'What time?' she asked.

'Seven?'

'I'll be there.'

'Good.' He stripped off the boiler suit and tried not to

think about how much he'd like to strip the boiler suit from her, too. To take off the rest of her clothes, very slowly, and touch her and taste her until she was going as crazy as he was. 'Can you recommend a laundry service?'

'Don't worry, it'll go in with the rest of the overalls.' She took it from him. 'See you later.'

Dinner with Felix.

Daisy knew she could always borrow another dress from Alexis, but that would involve explanations. As would borrowing high heels. She couldn't ask Annie, for the same reason. She was finding it hard to explain to herself, let alone to her best friend and her sister-in-law. In the end, she compromised with the outfit she normally wore for her presentations to schoolchildren: smart black trousers, a plain cream, strappy top, a bright red cardigan and plain, well-polished black loafers. At least business dress might help to keep her mind on business and not on how beautiful Felix's mouth was—or on wondering how it would feel if he followed through on that sugges-tion and traced a line of kisses along her collarbone.

I find you attractive—and I think it's mutual...

He was too perceptive for her liking. It was defi-nitely mutual. What was it about him that had her feeling so mixed up inside, longing for him and yet wanting to run a mile in the opposite direction at the same time?

When she walked into the reception area, Felix was waiting for her in one of the leather wing-backed arm-chairs. He was wearing a suit and white shirt, but for once he wasn't wearing a tie. It made him look a hun-dred times more approachable. Touchable.

She really should've said no. Made excuses. Done anything rather than turn up here to see him.

'Ready for dinner?' he asked.

She nodded, though the idea of eating with him on his balcony made her heart thud so hard that it drowned out any words in her head.

He ushered her over to the lift. It was as opulent as the rest of the hotel, with carpet you could sink into, recessed lighting in beautifully carved panelling and a very discreet mirror. As the doors closed behind them, they were completely alone.

Would Felix kiss her?

When he didn't, she wasn't sure whether she was more relieved or disappointed.

Clearly her confusion showed, because he reminded her softly, 'I said *dinner*, Boots,' as he opened the door to his suite and led her out to the balcony.

The table was set for two and there was a bottle of wine in a cooler, along with a jug of iced water.

'I hope you don't mind me ordering for you,' he said.

Actually, she did mind, and she was about to say so when he added, 'It's a tasting menu.'

'I had no idea they did one here.' Otherwise it would definitely have featured in her family's birthday cele-brations. The rest of the Bell clan appreciated good food as much as she did.

Felix smiled. 'The chef's a nice guy.'

She felt her eyes widen. She'd mentioned a tasting menu to him the first night they'd eaten together. And he'd acted on her suggestion? 'You mean you talked him into doing this tonight? Just for us?'

'You've taught me something, Daisy—people who do what they love also enjoy sharing it with others. Like you and the fairground.'

'But the chef here has two Michelin stars.'

Felix laughed. 'They don't all swear a lot and throw pans at people, you know. And actually he's been thinking about doing tasting menus for a while. He thinks it's a fabulous idea, and we're his guinea pigs. In return I promised we'd make notes.'

'You're being Mr Fixit again, aren't you?' she asked with a smile.

He wrinkled his nose. 'Pots and kettles, Boots. If you'd thought of it first, you would've gone to talk to him.'

'Maybe.'

'Come and eat with me, Daisy.' He smiled at her. 'This is going to be fun.'

And it was. A huge silver dome covered each platter; there were three different dishes in each. Until pudding: then there were five.

'Oh, *yes*. These are mine, all mine,' Daisy said, pulling the platter towards her.

'In your dreams, Boots. I love panna cotta.' Felix lifted his long-stemmed spoon and eyed her thoughtfully. 'Does this mean we have to have a spoon-fight to see who gets what?'

'What, a pen-pusher challenging an engineer?' She rolled her eyes. 'Then I'll have to make it fair and fight you with the spoon in my left hand. Though I'll still win, so you might as well surrender right now.'

'I have a much better idea,' Felix said. 'Close your eyes.'

'So you can scoff the lot while I'm waiting for my turn? No chance.'

'I'll let you have first taste of each dish.' He shifted his chair so that he was next to her rather than opposite her. 'Close your eyes and open your mouth.'

'Really?'

'Trust me,' he said softly, and she had a feeling he was talking about more than just the food.

She closed her eyes and opened her mouth. Felix fed her the first spoonful, the most sublime vanilla panna cotta she'd ever eaten.

'Good?' he asked.

'Yes.' To the food *and* the delivery. 'More than good.'

He made no comment, just poured them both a coffee and added milk to his own.

There was a platter of tiny hand-made chocolates to go with the coffee. 'Given the way you drink your coffee, I take it I have to surrender all the plain chocolate to you?' he asked.

She shook her head. 'No, though I'd be very happy to take the white chocolate off your hands.'

He smiled. 'White chocolate isn't even chocolate, so you're on. And we'll share the milk.'

'Sounds good to me.'

Except he insisted on feeding her the chocolates, too, one by one. By the time he'd finished, she was practically melting.

And then he kissed her, his mouth warm and sweet, yet tasting of bitter chocolate at the same time. Demanding and coaxing at the same time. Daisy had never felt so turned on in her entire life.

'Uh. This wasn't meant to…' Felix shook his head, trying to clear it. How had he managed to forget himself so thoroughly? How come Daisy was sitting on his lap? And why were his palms flat against her midriff, touching her bare skin?

Colour flooded Daisy's face and she took her hands away from his neck. 'Sorry.'

Oh, hell. Please don't say those are tears in her eyes. Except she was looking down, so her lashes obscured his view.

He'd clearly embarrassed her, made her feel bad. And he hated that. So when she began to wriggle off his lap he put his hand on her shoulder, stilling her. 'Daisy. It wasn't you. It's my fault.'

She still refused to look at him. 'It's OK. I understand.'

Understand what? Right at that moment Felix didn't understand a thing.

'I'll, um, call a taxi when I get downstairs.'

'Don't go. Not like this.' He sighed and rested his forehead against her shoulder. 'I apologise for pushing you. But sharing chocolates with you like that…I'm sorry. I should've kept my hands off you. But there's something about you I find irresistible, Daisy.' Despite his good intentions, he nuzzled her cardigan aside and kissed the bare skin of her shoulder. 'This sort of thing doesn't happen to me.'

'Why not?'

The question took him by surprise and he lifted his head again, looking her straight in the eye. 'I'm not with you.'

'Looking the way you do, you must have women dropping at your feet the whole time.'

Not for his looks. Felix knew the main reason why women were attracted to him, and it involved his net worth. Tabitha had burned that particular lesson into his soul. *I love the lifestyle he can give me.* But she hadn't loved him. He felt his mouth compress. 'Hardly.'

She scoffed. 'You honestly expect me to believe that? One charming smile from you, and most women would be a puddle of hormones.'

'Except you.' He traced the outline of her jaw with his forefinger. 'Because you're not most women.'

'I don't do feminine and fluffy.'

'That's not what I meant. Not at all.' He shook his head in exasperation. 'This is ridiculous. I'm meant to be good with words; I see through all the jargon and the hype and I summarise things neatly. And yet, with you, I can't think straight.' He dragged in a breath. 'All I can think of is that I want you. Very, very much. And I think you want me, too.'

She shivered. 'Yes.' Her voice was husky, and he wanted to see her sea-green eyes all drowsy and huge with pleasure. Pleasure that he'd given her.

'Having you close to me like this is driving me crazy.' Unable to help himself, he traced the line of her collar-bone with the tip of his finger. Except touching wasn't enough. Remembering what he'd wanted to do on Monday night, he bent his head and skimmed the hollows with his mouth. 'Daisy, your skin's so soft. And I'm really glad you're not wearing that necklace.'

'That was borrowed, too,' she admitted. She was trembling slightly. 'I don't do this sort of thing, Felix. I don't have mad, crazy affairs. I'm sensible Daisy Bell, who spends her day fixing engines covered in oil.'

'Just for the record, Boots,' he said softly, 'I don't do mad, crazy affairs, either. I'm usually sensible Felix Gisbourne, who spends his days looking at balance sheets and observing how companies function and where they could improve their performance. Sure, I date a bit.'

'A *bit*?' She looked as if she didn't believe him. Maybe she'd looked him up on the Internet, seen a few gossip columns.

'OK, I date a lot,' he clarified. 'But nothing serious. And I don't leap into bed with someone I've known for all of three days. This is going way too fast.'

'So we really ought to stop this right now.'

'Yes. Though I have a feeling that this thing is bigger than both of us.'

'So what do you suggest?'

'Neither of us is committed elsewhere. So there's nothing to stop us seeing where this takes us. And yes, I know we're supposed to be talking business, working out a rescue plan for the fairground. But we're adults, Daisy. We can make it strictly business at the fairground, and whatever this thing is between us outside.'

'Can we?' She didn't sound so sure.

He kissed the corner of her mouth. 'Maybe neither of us is in a fit state to make decisions right now. So let's be sensible. Right now, you're going to sit in that chair over there and I'm going to call a taxi for you. And tomorrow we're going to talk about the best way of getting this mad, crazy stuff out of our systems and our working life back to how it should be. Back in control.'

Though even as he spoke he thought he knew what the answer was.

A hot, no-strings affair, or a series of very long, cold showers.

CHAPTER SEVEN

ON THURSDAY morning, Daisy cycled in early and dropped in by the café to offer to do the tea run. She kept Felix—who was using her office for the day—until last.

'I thought it was about time I brought you a mug of tea, as you've brought me some for the last couple of days.'

'Thank you.' He smiled at her, and heat coiled in her belly. It would be oh, so easy to walk round to his side of the desk, sit on his lap and slide her hands round his neck, just as she'd done last night. To kiss him until they were both breathless and their heads were spinning.

His eyes darkened slightly; his gaze dropped to her mouth, and she knew he was thinking exactly the same thing.

But Bill was in the office next to hers. There wasn't a lock on her door. And it would involve way too many difficult explanations if someone walked in and found them wrapped in a clinch. They had to be sensible about this.

She took a deep breath. 'So have you come to a decision?'

'About what?'

She narrowed her eyes at him. 'What we were discussing.'

FREE BOOKS OFFER

To get you started, we'll send you
2 FREE books and a FREE gift

- -

There's no catch, everything is **FREE**

Accepting your 2 **FREE** books and **FREE** mystery gift
places you under no obligation to buy anything.

Be part of the Mills & Boon® Book Club™ and receive your favourite
Series books up to 2 months before they are in the shops and delivered
straight to your door. Plus, enjoy a wide range of **EXCLUSIVE** benefits!

- Best new women's fiction – delivered right to
  your door with FREE P&P

- Avoid disappointment – get your books up to
  2 months before they are in the shops

- No contract – no obligation to buy

We hope that after receiving your free books you'll
want to remain a member. But the choice is yours.
So why not give us a go? You'll be glad you did!

Visit **millsandboon.co.uk** to stay up to date
with offers and to sign-up for our newsletter

2 **FREE** books
and a
FREE gift

P0CIA

Mrs/Miss/Ms/Mr _____ Initials _____

BLOCK CAPITALS PLEASE

Surname _____

Address _____

_____

Postcode _____

Email _____

The Mills & Boon® Book Club™ – Here's how it works:

Accepting your free books places you under no obligation to buy anything. You may keep the books and gift and return the despatch note marked "cancel". If we do not hear from you, about a month later we'll send you 4 brand new books priced at £3.19* each. That is the complete price – there is no extra charge for post and packaging. You may cancel at any time, otherwise we will send you 4 stories a month which you may purchase or return to us – the choice is yours.

*Terms and prices subject to change without notice.

MILLS & BOON
Book Club

FREE BOOK OFFER
FREEPOST NAT 10298
RICHMOND
TW9 1BR

NO STAMP
NECESSARY
IF POSTED IN
THE U.K. OR N.I.

'The fairground? Not yet. I want to work through some figures and ideas.'

Oh, for pity's sake. He knew *exactly* what she was talking about. She lowered her voice. 'Do I have to spell it out for you?'

His eyes darkened still further and he moistened his lower lip. 'The crazy stuff. Yeah, I've thought about it. And, no, I haven't got a solution.'

'I thought you were meant to be Mr Fixit?'

'So did I,' he said dryly. 'Clearly today I've failed.'

'We could try avoiding each other.'

'That's not going to work,' he said.

She knew he was right, and it annoyed her. 'Do you have a better idea, then?'

'Oh, I have an idea, all right.' His eyes glittered. 'But I'm not looking for a relationship. I can't offer you something with a future. And, if anyone made the kind of suggestion that's in my head to one of my sisters, I would insist on having a little chat with them.'

She frowned. 'Don't you think your sisters are capable of dealing with things themselves?'

'Yes. But I'm their brother.'

'That's sexist.' And exactly how her brothers would react.

'No. It's called looking out for my sisters and making sure nobody takes advantage of them,' he countered. 'I was brought up to have good manners. And what I have in mind *isn't* good manners.'

A fling, she guessed. The same kind of deal he'd offered his other girlfriends.

Except he wasn't offering it to her, because she wasn't like them. Wasn't feminine enough.

Why can't you be like other girls? The words echoed

in her head. From her parents, her brothers, her boy-friends. She was too independent, too different.

It took every bit of willpower she possessed to drawl, 'Whatever. I have work to do. Catch you later.'

So much for trying to do the right thing and not hurt her, Felix thought ruefully. He'd managed to hurt her anyway. He'd seen it in her eyes.

He replayed their conversation in his head, and he still couldn't work it out. He'd tried to be honourable. What was wrong with that?

He'd talk to her later, find out what he'd said and apologise for it. But brooding over things wasn't going to sort out the paperwork or give him the information he needed to make suggestions about how to save the fairground.

But it was still niggling at him even after a morning's work on figures and several long conversations on his mobile phone. Time to declare a truce, he thought, and he dropped by the café to buy brownies before heading for the workshop.

He couldn't hear any singing as he walked into the workshop. Bill had said that was a bad sign. So he'd really upset her—but that hadn't been his intention at all.

Titan looked hopefully at the paper bag.

'Not for you today, boy,' Felix said, and scratched the cat behind the ears with his free hand. 'Can you fish her out for me?'

At the word 'fish', Titan gave a grumpy-sounding miaow, but did his usual duty.

'Can I help you?' Daisy said coolly when she emerged, keeping the engine between them.

'Peace offering.' He handed her the bag.

She looked inside and raised an eyebrow. 'Thank you.'

'Look, Daisy, I didn't intend to upset you this morning. I was trying not to insult you.'

'Uh-huh.'

He sighed. 'I'm not a mind-reader, Boots. What did I say?'

She lifted her chin. 'Nothing.'

'That's what my sisters say when they're seriously annoyed. It drives me crazy.' He leaned on the engine. 'Well, it's your choice. You can continue being hurt and angry, or you can tell me what I said and I can apologise for it. Up to you.'

She was silent, but eventually she bit her lip. 'You were going to suggest a fling.'

'And, as I said, I was trying not to insult you. That's why I didn't suggest it.'

'So it wasn't…' Her voice tailed off.

'Wasn't what?'

'Nothing.' She flapped a hand. 'You're right. Better to be sensible. And I don't really mix with suits.'

Then it hit him. She had the same look on her face as she'd had the evening before, when he'd kissed her and stopped.

She didn't think she was his type. She thought he was rejecting her.

'Daisy,' he said softly. 'Are you trying to tell me I don't think you're my type?'

'No.' But she hadn't looked him in the eye. He knew she wasn't telling the truth.

He walked round to her side of the engine. 'Right. Define my type.'

She still refused to meet his gaze. 'Elegant. Girly. The sort who doesn't have to borrow a dress to go to a posh hotel.'

In other words, the complete opposite of her. 'And you think I judge by appearances?'

She lifted her chin. 'Don't you?'

'No,' he said, unsmiling and annoyed that she'd read him so wrongly. 'I tend to look a little deeper. And, for the record, you don't have to wear a dress to be all woman. You manage to do that even when you're wearing a shapeless boiler suit and you've hidden your hair behind a cap.'

She looked surprised, and then gave him a disbelieving stare.

'I'm trying very hard to do the honourable thing here, but you're making this impossible for me. Because I can see in your face you think I'm spinning you a line, and I can think of only one way to prove to you that I'm not.' He cupped her face in his hands and brushed his mouth over hers, once, twice. And when her lips parted he traced a line of tiny, nibbling kisses along her lower lip, demanding a response.

She let him deepen the kiss, sliding her arms around his neck; his hands automatically went to her waist, settling in the perfect hourglass curve.

'Believe me now?' he asked when he finally lifted his head.

She looked dazed. 'Uh. Yes.'

'I'd guess,' he said softly, 'that someone—someone *very* stupid—did a number on you. And I'd also guess that he found your job threatening, and the only way he could feel good about himself was to put you down constantly. So he nagged you because you weren't wearing make-up and high heels like his friends' girlfriends did.'

She flinched—only slightly, but enough to tell him that he was right.

'He was wrong. Incredibly wrong. You're bright, and from what I've seen you're in the perfect job for you. You'd be bored stupid if you had to play housewife.' He couldn't help smiling. 'Though, judging by how untidy your office is, you'd need a housekeeper anyway.'

'I'm not that messy. And I know where everything is.'

'You work on the volcano principle—that when a piece of paper is critical it'll rise to the top of the pile.'

'And your problem with that is?'

'I'm a control freak.'

'The sort who has a clear desk policy.'

He laughed. 'I had to stop myself tidying your office this morning.'

She flushed. 'It's *my* office.'

'I know, so don't get territorial with me. I didn't touch anything. Even though I wanted to.' Which was precisely the dilemma he had where she was concerned. He wanted to touch. To taste. He drew the pad of his thumb along her lower lip. 'So what are we going to do about *this*?'

'Maybe…' She stopped.

'Maybe what?'

'Maybe,' she said slowly, 'you could have dinner with me tonight. At my place.'

If only she'd asked him earlier. 'Sorry, I can't. I'm going back to London this afternoon. I need to be in my office for a couple of days to sort some things out on other projects.' He'd made promises, and he never broke his word.

She gave an offhand shrug.

But Felix guessed that his refusal had hurt, that she thought he'd made up an excuse. And he had a feeling that she hadn't made that offer lightly. When it came to her personal life, Daisy was as wary as he was. 'I'm planning to be back in Suffolk on Sunday evening. Can I take a rain check on dinner for then, if you're not already busy?' he asked.

She looked at him for a moment, and then nodded. 'Sunday's fine.'

'What time?'

'Half-past seven?'

'OK. I'll see you when I get back.'

He was about to leave when she spoke. 'Um, Felix?' She waved a cloth at him. 'You might need this, and a mirror.'

'Mirror?'

She flapped a hand. 'Come here.' Carefully, she wiped something—a smudge of oil, he guessed—from his face.

'Thank you. Until Sunday, then.'

'Until Sunday.'

On Friday, Felix was at his desk, but he couldn't settle. Something kept nagging at him. Even two espressos didn't help him concentrate.

And then he realised what it was.

He missed Daisy.

Which was utterly ridiculous. He'd known her for less than a week, and had seen her less than twenty-four hours ago. How could he possibly be missing her?

But he was. He missed the sparkle of fencing with her. And, even though his head told him that these few days back in London away from her would be good for him and give his common sense the chance of returning, there was another feeling deep in his gut. One that begged to differ.

Maybe he just needed some fresh air to clear his

head. Somehow his walk led him past the local choco-latier. A note in the window said that they could ice any message onto any slab of chocolate. Acting on impulse, Felix went inside.

'Would it be possible to ice a picture instead of a message?' he asked.

'Sure.' The girl behind the counter gave him an ap-preciative smile, and leaned forward slightly.

Felix barely registered that it deepened her cleavage or that she was flirting with him. 'And could you send it by courier so it arrives tomorrow?'

'No problem.'

'And I'd like to put a message in as well.'

'Of course, sir.'

'Wonderful.' He told her exactly what he wanted iced on the slab, paid, scribbled a quick message on the back of a business card, and gave her Daisy's address at the fairground.

On Saturday morning, Bill came over to the workshop from the office. 'Special delivery for you.'

Daisy couldn't remember ordering anything. Frown-ing, she cleaned her hands and opened the box. It con-tained a large slab of white chocolate that had an old-fashioned roundabout iced on it in milk chocolate, with little red dots for the lights; it was the most charming thing she'd ever seen.

There was a business card attached: Felix.

Suddenly, all her pleasure evaporated. He'd sent her the most lovely gift—and he'd even remembered that white chocolate was her favourite—but he hadn't sent a message with it. Just a business card. Which she supposed was a kind of message in itself: he'd had time to think about things and thought they should keep it strictly business between them.

He'd probably even got his secretary to organise the chocolate, rather than doing it himself. He had a busy schedule, after all. This wasn't personal, and it was stupid of her to have hoped. Stupid of her to have missed him. Stupid of her to think that maybe he'd see her for herself.

'What's this, something you were thinking of stocking in the shop?' Bill asked, looking interested.

She showed him the chocolate and forced her voice to sound neutral. 'Felix sent it. And it's a good idea—something like this would go down well in the shop, though I think we should make smaller ones to keep the price in pocket-money ranges.'

'Agreed,' Bill said. 'As it's white chocolate, I assume none of us are going to get a look in?'

Eating it would choke her. But she made herself laugh, for Bill's sake. She didn't want him worrying about her on top of everything else. 'I'm not quite that greedy, Bill. Take it back to the office and share it out, but make sure you leave me some, OK? And I'll text him to say we like the idea.'

She dropped Felix's business card as she took the mobile phone from her handbag, and it fell face-down; there was something written on the back. She picked it up and read the message: *Saw this and thought of you. Fx*

So he'd organised this himself, not delegated it.

The only question was, did he mean 'you' as in Daisy herself, or 'you' as in the fairground?

On impulse, rather than texting him, she rang him.

'Gisbourne.'

He sounded all buttoned-up again. Not the man who fenced verbally with her, or the man whose kiss had fried her brain. It made her wish she'd stuck to her original plan to text him her thanks. Too late, now. 'Hi, it's Daisy. I won't keep you. I just wanted to say thank you for the chocolate. Bill agrees it'd be great in the shop, but we think a smaller size would work better.'

'Good decision,' he said, his voice still cool.

She really had done the wrong thing here. 'Sorry for interrupting. I'll let you get on.'

'Daisy, no, wait.'

'What?'

He sighed. 'I didn't send it for the fairground. I sent it to *you*. I thought you'd like it.'

Suddenly there was a huge lump in her throat. It had been a message. Only she'd been paranoid and decoded it wrongly.

'Daisy? Are you there?'

'Yeah. Um, thanks. I did like it. A lot.' She dragged in a breath and forced herself to sound professional. 'I won't keep you, though. See you tomorrow.'

'Half-past seven, right?'

Her heart skipped a beat. 'Half-past seven.'

On Sunday, Daisy was working in her office when there was a rap on the door.

She glanced up and saw Felix. He looked absolutely edible in black trousers, an open-necked shirt with the sleeves rolled up and a pair of dark glasses.

For one mad moment, she considered getting up and throwing herself into his arms, but she knew it would make him back off again, so she stayed where she was.

'Hi. You look like—' *any woman's dream come true* '—a tourist.'

'I am.' He smiled at her. 'Hello.'

'Hello.'

'It's one o'clock,' he said.

'Uh-huh.'

'And, knowing you, you haven't had a break yet.'

'I'm fine. I'll grab a sandwich at my desk later.'

'Wrong. You're taking a break right now.'

'Bossing me about now?' she asked.

'No, you have a choice. You can come with me quietly, or you can come with me kicking and screaming. Bottom line: you're leaving this room for forty-five minutes.'

'Thirty.'

'Forty-five.'

He was utterly implacable, and Daisy judged it politic to give in. She let him shepherd her over to the café, where he collected sandwiches and fruit for them; she sat with him at the picnic tables while they ate, enjoying the sunshine, and she gave in to his suggestion to wander round the fairground. 'It's work,' he said. 'We're checking that the customers are happy. Seeing what they like and what they don't like.'

She'd told him that the gondola was her favourite ride, so she wasn't surprised when he made her queue up there with him. The ride was really popular, so she had to sit next to him in the car rather than opposite him. And she felt his fingers lace through hers—discreetly, because their hands were hidden from sight, but he was holding her hand. Staking his claim.

'We've been apart for three days,' he said conversationally. 'Which should have been long enough for us to get our common sense back.'

Yet he was right next to her, holding her hand. 'So have you?' she asked. 'Got your common sense back, I mean?'

'No.' He gave her a wry smile. 'Have you?'

'No.'

'Then maybe we should try the other way of getting it out of our system,' he said.

She swallowed hard; her stomach was a knot of nerves. 'So you're suggesting an affair.'

'I'm suggesting we explore this thing between us.'

'For how long?'

He shrugged. 'As long as it takes to get it out of our systems.'

'And the fairground?' she asked carefully.

'Is a completely separate matter. This is just between you and me.'

She took a deep breath. 'Starting when?'

'This dinner you had planned for tonight…could we do it tomorrow?'

She nodded.

'Then I'll pick you up tonight. We'll have dinner. Walk on the beach.'

It was what he hadn't said that made a shiver of pure pleasure run down her spine: what would happen after they'd walked on the beach.

Though one thing bothered her. 'So it starts at your hotel.'

'Neutral territory,' he said.

That made sense, but she still needed to know. 'What's wrong with my place?'

'Nothing. But you live in a small village. People will notice if my car is parked outside your house all evening; they'll start speculating, asking questions. And I'd rather this was just between us.'

She bit her lip. 'What time?'

'Half-past seven. If that gives you enough time to do whatever you need to do.'

Cycle home, shower, change, feed Titan. 'Yes.' She took a deep breath. 'So, if we're going to your hotel, I have to wear a dress.'

He smiled. 'No. Wear whatever you like. We can walk first, then eat on my balcony, if you'd rather.'

His balcony.

Last time, they'd ended up kissing each other stupid, and they'd just about been able to stop.

This time, they didn't have to stop. Adrenaline flooded through her at the thought. 'That's fine,' she said, her voice very slightly cracked.

'Then,' he said softly, 'it's a date.'

CHAPTER EIGHT

AT HALF-PAST seven precisely, Felix rang the doorbell. Daisy answered, looking just a little flustered.

'I can come back if you need more time,' he said.

'No, it's fine.'

She'd changed, he noticed. Into smart black trousers, a black top and a bright red cardigan. 'You look lovely,' he said.

'Thank you.'

She also looked as nervous as he felt. Crazy. Tonight had been his idea: he was in control, so there was no reason why he should feel nervous. No reason why adrenaline should be skittering through his veins.

He waited for her to lock her front door, then opened the passenger door for her. Once they were back at the hotel, he shepherded her over to the beach. The sun had started to drop below the horizon and the sea was calm, the waves swishing gently onto the shore.

'Want to paddle?' he asked.

She shook her head. 'I'm not really dressed for it.'

He could imagine her in bare feet and a pair of cut-off jeans. Or very, very short shorts. His mouth went dry. 'Uh-huh.'

She gave him a sidelong look. 'And I can't see *you* paddling. You might get messy.'

That made him blink. 'You think I'm scared of mess?'

'You're a control freak, Felix. Everything's neat and tidy in your world.'

There was nothing tidy about the way he was feeling right now. Nothing compartmentalised. Just a ratcheting of tension. A mixture of urgent need and desire, combined with worry that this was going to be a huge mistake for both of them. But, for the life of him, he couldn't think of another solution, any other way to get her out of his system. 'Not everything,' he said.

'No?' Her expression called him a big, fat liar. 'Prove it.'

He stopped dead, spun her into his arms and kissed her. It was hot, open-mouthed and intense. And she kissed him back, as she had that night by her borrowed car, demanding and offering in equal measure.

When he finally broke the kiss, they were both quivering.

'Was that untidy enough for you?' he asked.

Her eyes had darkened to jade. 'Yes.'

Now.

He could see it in her face, the same need that thrummed through him. He let his hands slide down her arms, twined his fingers through hers, and walked back to the hotel. Through the lobby. Into the lift. Neither of them said a word as the doors swished together and the lift glided up to the third floor. But Felix was looking at her mouth, and when he glanced up for a second he could see that she was staring at his mouth, too.

Wanting.

Needing.

It was getting harder and harder to breathe as the lift doors opened and he walked with her to his door. He slid the card key into the lock, making a huge effort not to let his hands shake, even though he was as tense as hell.

Then the door closed behind them and she was in his arms.

His mouth was jammed over hers, she was kissing him back as if she couldn't slake her thirst for him. He had no idea who started undressing who, but somehow they were standing by his bed. Daisy was naked apart from a pair of white lacy knickers, his shirt was he didn't care where, and she was struggling to undo the button of his trousers.

So much for his reputation as a lover with finesse.

He was behaving as if he were eighteen and making love for the first time.

Hell, he *felt* as if he were eighteen and making love for the first time.

He needed to slow this down. For both their sakes. But then Daisy trailed her fingers over his chest, forcing him to reciprocate by cupping her breasts, and the sheer perfection of her curves was just too much for him.

He dropped to his knees in front of her and drew one nipple into his mouth. Daisy gave a sigh of pleasure and tipped her head back, sliding her hands into his hair. She was so responsive to his touch, and Felix loved it. Loved the fact that he could turn this bright, sassy woman into pure mush. He kissed the soft undersides of her breasts, then moved lower over her midriff and skated kisses round her navel. He breathed in her scent; it reminded him of summer berries. Which was about right: she tasted like a lush, summer afternoon, and he wanted more. A lot more. He wanted to make her head spin, the way she did his. He wanted to touch her and taste her and ease his body inside hers. He wanted to see her eyes all drowsy with pleasure, sated with his lovemaking.

And he wanted it all *now*.

He slid one hand between her thighs, and she quivered. 'Felix.' His name was a hiss of pleasure.

He cupped her sex; he could feel heat radiating from her, the same heat that fizzed through his own body. Slowly, gently, he pushed the lacy material aside. Slid one finger along her sex. Brushed her clitoris once, twice. She whimpered and her fingers tightened in his hair. 'Yes. Oh, yes.' She widened her stance slightly, offering, and he took the hint, pushing a finger inside her and shifting his hand so the base of his thumb rubbed against her clitoris.

Felix loved the way her breathing changed, becoming quicker and more shallow as her arousal grew. He teased her until he could feel her body quivering with tension. Then, and only then, he stood up, picked her up and laid her against the pillows. Stripped off the rest of his clothing in two seconds flat. Slowly, slowly he peeled down her knickers, maintaining eye contact the whole time. Daisy blushed deeply, but her eyes were pure jade, telling him she was just as turned on as he was.

He lifted her leg and kissed the hollows of her ankle, still looking straight into her eyes, then nibbled his way down her calf to the back of her knee. Her hands had fisted in his sheets, and he could see how uneven her breathing was. Just to prolong the torment, he made his way very, very slowly along her thigh. And then he shifted so he could draw his tongue along the length of her sex. So very, very slowly.

Daisy moaned aloud and tipped her head back against his pillows, arching her body to give him better access. He teased her clitoris with the tip of his tongue until she was starting to quiver, then pushed a finger inside her. He felt her fingers slide into his hair, urging him on, and then he heard her give a surprised, 'Oh!' of pleasure and felt her body ripple round him.

He kissed his way back up to her mouth. 'That was for you,' he said quietly.

'Felix, I...' She stroked his face, clearly near to tears. 'Thank you.'

'My pleasure.' He kissed her lightly. 'But I haven't finished yet. Not by a long way. This time's for both of us.' He retrieved his wallet from his trousers and removed a condom; he ripped the foil packet open and rolled it on before kneeling between her thighs again.

'OK?' he asked softly, checking; even though it would be hell for him to stop now, he needed to be sure she wanted this as much as he did.

When she nodded, he fitted the tip of his penis against her and slowly, slowly eased inside. Deeper and deeper. Until he was completely sheathed inside her and her legs were wrapped round his waist.

Pure, unadulterated bliss.

Daisy had guessed that Felix would be good at this, but she'd also underestimated him. She really hadn't expected him to be such a generous lover, thinking of her pleasure first. Making her feel cherished. Special.

She arched her back and drew him deeper.

'That's good,' Felix said, his voice deeper and huskier than she remembered. 'You feel so good, Daisy.'

'So do you,' she whispered shakily. The perfect fit.

It shouldn't be like this, the first time. It should be awkward and a bit ungainly, with neither of them knowing how to please the other and having to work on a best-guess scenario.

But this was amazing. As if they were already in tune.

Either Felix was extremely practised, or this was something special. Right at that moment, she couldn't tell which.

He kissed her hard, and then he began to move, varying the pace and pressure of his thrusts until he found a rhythm that made her breathing quicken. Unbelievably, she felt warmth coil tighter and tighter within her. No way had she ever come twice, so close together before.

She was at the point of hyperventilating when her climax hit her. 'Felix.' His name was a sigh of sheer delight.

Then he stilled, focused and completely lost in pleasure, before giving her a sweet kiss that felt as if it touched her somewhere deep inside.

He dealt with the condom, then drew her back into his arms.

Odd how it felt so comfortable to be with him, not needing words. She enjoyed sparring with him, yet being quiet with him was good, too. Right now, there was no need to fill the silence.

Then her stomach rumbled.

She closed her eyes, feeling embarrassed colour flood into her face. 'I'm sorry.'

'My fault. I was supposed to feed you first.'

'We can't go down to dinner. I don't know where my clothes are.'

He laughed and propped himself on his elbow, looking down at her. 'I don't know where most of mine

are, either.' He stole a kiss. 'I'll go hunt them down. And
you can think about what you'd like to eat so I can order
room-service.'

'Felix, I can't believe we just…' She bit her lip. 'And
we hardly said a word to each other.'

He stroked her face. 'Talking wasn't exactly upper-
most in my mind. And I don't think it was in yours,
either.'

'No,' she admitted.

'Is it a problem?'

She wasn't sure. They were going to have to talk
about this at some point. Decide where they were
going from here.

'Look, there's a menu in the drawer. Choose whatever you like. But may I suggest you choose something
cold?'

'Cold?'

'In case,' he told her, his voice deepening, 'we get a
little bit distracted.'

She knew he meant if they ended up making love again
before they ate. Daisy felt her blush deepening. 'Felix!'

'You asked.' He shrugged, and gave her a wicked
grin. 'And meanwhile I'll find our clothes.' He slid off
the bed, still naked, completely unselfconscious.

Daisy couldn't take her eyes off him. Clothed, he was
beautiful. Naked, he was magnificent. Broad shoulders
and flat abs that told her he worked out regularly, and a
truly delectable backside.

She was still thinking about him, not even having retrieved the menu, when he walked in with a pile of
clothes—his and hers, tangled together.

Just as their bodies had been.

'Have you decided what you'd like yet?' he asked.

You. 'Um…sorry.'

He gave her a truly wicked smile, dropped the clothes on the bed and fished the room-service menu out of a drawer. 'Here. Have a read.'

Except she couldn't resist watching him as he folded their clothes neatly and put them on a chair. She was still very aware that they were both naked. That they'd made love. And once wasn't nearly enough.

When he'd finished, he sat down beside her. 'So, what would you like?'

'What would you suggest?' she fenced, not wanting to admit that her concentration had failed her yet again.

He kissed the spot just behind her ear. 'Lots of things. But I promised to feed you first. How about I order us a chicken salad and we take a shower while we're waiting?'

'Sounds good.'

Showering with Felix was sheer pleasure. Daisy enjoyed soaping him all over, learning the curves of his body and just where he liked being touched. And she enjoyed it even more when he explored her in turn.

They'd just started dressing when there was a knock at the door.

Felix grabbed a cashmere sweater from his wardrobe and pulled it on, zipping up his trousers as he walked out of the bedroom door and closed it behind him. By the time he rapped on the door and peered round it, she'd finished dressing.

'Dinner is served, madam,' he said with a smile, and ushered her out to his balcony.

There was even a vanilla-scented candle burning in the centre of the table; sitting watching the sky as it faded into darkness was just wonderful.

'This is lovely, Felix,' she said.

'Sorry, I should have asked you—did you want some wine?'

'No, but don't let me stop you.'

'I'm driving you home,' he said.

Oh. So he wasn't going to ask her to stay. She was annoyed with herself for feeling disappointed; what had she expected? This was a mad fling, designed to get it out of their systems. It wasn't the beginning of a relationship. So she should be feeling relieved. This was an affair with defined limits, and neither of them was going to get hurt.

The food was fabulous, but best of all was the pudding: white chocolate and raspberry crème brûlée, one of the nicest she'd ever tasted. 'Felix Gisbourne, you're such a hedonist,' she said.

'You finished yours first,' he pointed out.

His eyes were very dark, and his expression was unfathomable. She had no idea what he was thinking, what he was feeling.

Nothing for it but to bite the bullet.

'So, the crazy stuff,' she said, lifting her chin and trying to be brave. 'All OK now?'

'That depends what you mean by OK,' he said.

'Is it out of your system?'

'Is it out of yours?'

No. But she didn't want to sound needy. 'I asked first.'

He smiled wryly. 'Not quite.'

Time to compromise. 'Me, neither. So what happens now?'

'Up to you. We can stop. Or…'

Her chest felt tight. 'Or?'

'We explore this. See where it takes us. But it's just between you and me.'

She knew it was the sensible thing; neither of them was ready to share this with the outside world. Neither of them knew where it was going. Keeping it to themselves would avoid any pressure. Yet part of her still hurt. Part of her still wondered: was it going to be like it had been with her exes, with him thinking she wasn't feminine enough?

She let out a yelp of surprise as Felix scooped her out of her chair and settled her on his lap, wrapping his arms round her waist. 'Felix!'

'You're brooding. What's the problem?'

'Nothing.'

He coughed. 'Like to rephrase that?'

'It's…' She sighed. 'No, it's nothing. You're right. This takes all the pressure off. It saves my family grilling you about your intentions.'

'Your family would grill me?'

'My mother thinks I'm firmly on the shelf and that I'm never going to settle down. And she's desperate for grandchildren.'

'I thought Ben had children.'

'He does. But I'm her only daughter. She wants me settled.'

'Tell me about it,' he said feelingly. 'Mine's always holding house parties with a suitable woman she's picked especially as my dinner partner, hoping that I'll start dating.' He grimaced. 'Even though both my sisters are married, I'm the oldest and the only son. She thinks I should do my duty, get married and produce grandchildren.'

'But you don't want to get married?'

'I don't want to be trapped.' His voice was cool to the point of being arctic.

She frowned. 'What happened to you, Felix?'

He looked away. 'Nothing.'

Yeah, right. That was about as sincere as her own 'nothing'. Just before he'd looked away, she'd seen something in his eyes. A bone-deep hurt.

Something or someone had made him scared of marriage.

He'd said he was single—divorced, maybe? It would explain why he saw marriage as a trap.

But she also knew that if she pushed right now he'd shut her out. So she waited for him to fill the silence.

'Not everyone wants to settle down,' Felix said eventually. 'What's wrong with having a little fun? Aren't you the woman who's dedicating her life to putting a bit of fun and sparkle into families' lives?'

'Absolutely. And I don't want to get married, either.' She'd been asked. By a man who hadn't seen her for herself. Stu had seen a woman who he'd thought just needed a shove in the right direction and a wedding dress, and she'd be more conventional. Girly.

'Then,' he said, 'I vote for fun. You, me and a good time. Until one of us has had enough.'

'Until one of us has had enough,' she echoed.

CHAPTER NINE

IN THE middle of Monday afternoon, Titan did his guard-dog routine and Daisy emerged from under the engine to face Felix.

'Hi,' she said, a little unsure how to act. He'd said that they could keep things compartmentalised—so what was he doing here? Was this business…? That glint in his eyes made her toes curl. It was all she could do to stop herself wrapping her arms round his neck and kissing him. Deeply.

He smiled at her. 'I need you for a meeting.'

'A meeting?'

'With Bill,' he clarified.

'So you've come to a decision about the fairground?'

'That's why we're having a meeting,' he said.

He was giving nothing away. 'Remind me never to play poker against you,' she said lightly.

'Chicken.' He moved closer and stole a kiss. 'Come on, Boots. Let's get this show on the road.'

If it was a no to the investment, he wouldn't sound so cool and calm and collected, would he?

Daisy really couldn't tell. So she cleaned her hands and followed him over to the office. Bill had a plate of brownies in his office and he'd put the kettle on; Daisy elected to make the coffee, because she couldn't stand the suspense and needed something to do with her hands.

When she carried the mugs into Bill's office, Felix gestured to the spare seat.

'We all know why I'm here, so let's cut to the chase. I've spent a week here and looked round thoroughly. Your staff are great—they know what your customers want and they give it,' he said. 'The concept of the museum works because it's unusual and it fits in with the local tourism. The management is fine.'

There was a single word he hadn't said. One that showed in his eyes. So Daisy said it for him. 'But?'

'You need to make some changes if you want to maximise your revenue. It's a matter of using your resources better. As we've already discussed at length, Daisy, you need to look at your pricing structure, and at having some kind of central hall so you have more flexibility and can offer activities for damp days as well as sunny ones to keep people coming in. And you need to offer merchandise through your website as well as in the shop.'

Bill jotted notes on a pad. 'So that's three main areas we need to look at.'

'You don't need to take notes, Bill,' Felix said quietly. 'I'll give you a report with my recommendations. And there's another one that might be really difficult to face but it needs discussing. The sooner, the better.'

Now that she hadn't expected. She exchanged a worried glance with Bill.

'What's that?' Bill asked.

'Succession planning. Bill, you need to think about what you want to do when you eventually retire. If you want Bell's to continue like this, then you need to talk to a solicitor about turning the museum from a private collection into a charitable trust—because, if you don't, when you die your heirs will have to pay tax on the inheritance, and that might mean having to liquidate some of the assets to pay for it.'

'You mean, sell one of the engines or one of the rides,' Daisy said.

'Exactly. And, with the way the economy is, people are putting money into tangibles and prices are rising—so that means the tax bill will rise, too.'

'Will your report also recommend investors?' Daisy asked.

'That depends. If you become a charity or a trust rather than a private collection, you'll qualify for grants and you'll find it easier to get sponsorship. You have a great bunch of volunteers, but I notice you don't actually have a "friends" scheme—people who run those kind of schemes are usually excellent at raising extra funds. You need that money to cover restoration costs and buying new rides.'

'And if we stay as we are and keep it a private collection?' Bill asked.

'Then you need an investor to bring in some extra funds to help you develop.'

'Or a sponsor,' Daisy said. Time to bite the bullet. 'Would you consider doing that?'

'If that's the route you choose to take, then I can help you work out sponsorship packages. What you need to do is talk it over between you, come to a decision and then talk to me. Obviously I have other projects to deal with, but I can split my time between here and London for the next month or so. Say,

Wednesday to Friday in London and the rest of the time here.'

'That would be wonderful,' Bill said.

And, when that month was up, what then? Would their relationship revert to being strictly business? Daisy wondered.

'The bottom line is,' Felix continued, 'Bell's has a future and you can tell everyone to stop worrying.'

Bill hugged Daisy, then shook Felix's hand solemnly. 'Thank you. You have no idea how much this means to us.'

Daisy, seeing the look in Felix's eyes, rather thought he might.

'I'll leave you to discuss things for now,' Felix said with a smile. 'I have a report to write, so I'll head back to the hotel and I'll see you tomorrow.' He glanced at Daisy. 'I'll give you a hand with the kitchen stuff before I go.'

In other words, he wanted a quiet word with her on her own. Her pulse beat just that little bit faster. 'Sure,' she said, aiming for cool and casual.

'Are you doing anything special tonight?' he asked when they were on their own.

'I don't have any plans. So, um, if you want to use that rain check on dinner at my place…'

'I'd like that.' He checked that nobody was around to see them, and stole a kiss. 'Text me a time when you get back to the workshop and I'll be there.'

She did so. And, as she expected, her doorbell rang dead on time. Felix had probably never been late for anything in his life.

'For you,' Felix said, handing her a bottle of chilled Chablis and some seriously good chocolates.

'Thank you.' It felt odd, inviting him into her inner sanctum. 'Come in.'

'Anything I can do to help?' he asked as she ushered him through to the kitchen.

'It's all done—but you can undo the wine, if you like.' She handed him a corkscrew; he removed the cork and poured them both a glass.

'To the fairground,' he said, lifting his glass.

'And to you,' she replied, lifting hers.

She took some dishes from the oven and transferred a piece of salmon to Titan's bowl.

'You cooked salmon for Titan, too?' he asked.

She grinned. 'I wouldn't dare not. Remember, this cat growls.' She scratched the top of his head. 'And he's seriously spoiled.'

Titan responded by purring and rubbing against her.

She checked the fish for bones, then mashed it. 'Now, you know you have to wait until it's cooled down before you can scoff it,' she told the cat. 'Patience.'

Titan gave a miaow of disgust and stalked over to his bed.

Daisy opened the rest of the foil-wrapped parcels from the oven and set asparagus, new potatoes and stuffed mushrooms next to them, then brought the plates over to the table.

'I thought you said you couldn't cook,' Felix commented.

She shrugged. 'Wrapping things in foil and shoving them in the oven isn't exactly cooking.'

'Works for me.' He smiled at her. 'I like your kitchen, Boots.'

'Thanks. I love my house, too. It might be small, but

it's perfect for me.' She gave him a wistful smile. 'I spent a lot of years in this kitchen, when I was growing up, talking to Granny Bell and listening to her tales of the fairground.'

'It was her house?' Felix guessed.

Daisy nodded. 'She left it to me—along with a letter. She said she'd helped my brothers through university and with their first car, and because I didn't go to university, and I'd put so much back into the fairground, this was her way of helping me.'

He raised an eyebrow. 'So you're proud?'

'Yes. No.' She sighed. 'I love my family. But you know how families are: there are dynamics and everyone has their set places. They see me as the ditzy, girly baby who needs rescuing. Which drives me insane, because that's not who I am.'

'So you wear boiler suits and you work with steam engines to prove you're not ditzy or girly or need rescuing.'

'Partly. But I love what I do.' She looked at him. 'So where are you in yours?'

'My family dynamics, you mean?' At her nod, he gave her a half-smile. 'I'm the difficult workaholic who refuses to do my duty and join the family firm, or settle down and produce the next generation of Gisbournes.'

Which told her exactly where she stood: though she knew that already. 'Hey. You know what they say—all work and no play.'

She'd expected him to tease her back, but instead Felix suddenly went quiet on her and concentrated on his food.

What had she said? Felix himself had admitted to being a workaholic. OK, so she'd come out with a cliché, but surely it hadn't been that bad? Part of her wanted to ask him what was wrong, but she had the distinct impression that he'd closed off and wouldn't tell her. Asking would make it worse.

She let it lie until they'd finished eating. 'Sorry. I'm not the world's best cook.'

'It was fine, Daisy. Really.' But he was avoiding her gaze.

She reached across the table and squeezed his hand. 'Felix, what I said earlier…I wasn't sniping at you. I'm always being nagged about my workaholic tendencies, too, and I hate it, so I guess it's the same for you.'

'Who nags you?'

'My parents. My brothers. My sister-in-law.' Her exes. Not that she wanted to talk about them. 'They say I should take days off.'

'You don't?' He frowned.

'I work part-time at the fairground as a mechanic. The office stuff is voluntary, and so's some of the restoration work.' She shrugged. 'But nobody forces me to do it. It's my heritage and it's important to me. And, thanks to you, I can continue doing what I love, and loving what I do.'

'Mmm-hmm.'

She really didn't understand why he'd clammed up on her. It wasn't as if she'd accused him outright of being dull. Besides, he wasn't dull. He was dynamic, bright and incredibly sexy, and surely he had to know that?

Unless…

A seriously nasty thought slid into her mind. Last night, they'd made an agreement: *until one of them had had enough.*

'Do I take it,' she asked carefully, 'that you've got your common sense back?'

He looked straight at her, his grey eyes guarded. 'Have you?'

She could be proud and say yes, make sure she was the one who ended it. But she had a feeling that there was something else going on here, something she didn't understand, and it might take a while to get to the bottom of it. 'No. I had been planning to introduce you to my sofa, actually. But, if you'd rather not, I understand.'

'You were going to introduce me to your sofa,' he repeated.

'On condition you don't nag me for being untidy,' she said.

'Now, would I?' He gave her the wickedest smile she'd ever seen.

The tension within her eased; the potential row had been averted. 'Hey. You're the one who has issues with my desk.'

'I can think of things I'd like to do on your desk. And all that paperwork would get in the way,' he said softly.

All kinds of ideas bloomed in her head, and she felt hot all over. 'Why don't you come and explain that to me on my sofa? Once I've fed the cat.' She checked the temperature of the salmon in Titan's bowl and finally set the bowl in front of the impatient cat before leading Felix into the living room. 'I did warn you I'm not tidy.'

Looking at it as she knew he'd see it, she could perceive the clutter: the papers on top of her map cabinet, the DVDs of musicals stacked on a shelf in no particular order. Felix, no doubt, would have them and the pile of books by the sofa organised in alphabetical order.

'I'm not saying a word, Boots,' he said softly. 'It's a nice room.'

'I like it.'

'Nice sofa.'

'Untidy sofa,' she admitted. There was a pile of

papers she'd been going through on one of the seats; she
scooped them up together with the notebook where
she'd been jotting down information and moved them
on to the top of the map cabinet.

'Work?' he asked.

'Sort of. Family papers. I'm thinking about writing
a history of Bell's, to supplement the fairground's guide-
book. Dad and Bill have lent me a pile of stuff, and there
are boxes of photographs that Granny Bell kept in the
attic.' She looked at Felix. 'She would've liked you.'

'What, even though I'm fussy?'

'She had a thing about neatness, too. I suppose it
came from travelling between fairs.'

'So your grandmother was a traveller?'

'No, she was a showman. There's a difference,' Daisy
said. 'Travellers go where the fancy takes them, whereas
showmen have things booked months if not years in
advance—they work the fair circuit, and the dates of
most of the fairs were set centuries ago. But, yes, they
lived in vans because they had to travel between fairs, and
those vans are full of cubby holes to keep things neat.'

'And you didn't inherit the family neatness.'

'Not where papers are concerned,' she admitted. 'But
my workshop's tidy.'

'Only to keep the health and safety mandarins off
your back. You prefer the engineering side to the admin
side, don't you?'

'Much. But I can't leave it all to Bill, so I do my fair
share.'

He played with the ends of her hair. 'Before I met you,
I decided you were a lightweight who drifted around,
was late for meetings and chatted up the mechanics.'

'Oh, yes?'

He dipped his head to brush his mouth against hers. 'Then Bill told me you were the chief mechanic, so I assumed you'd be butch, with a tattoo and a nose-ring—even though I'd seen your picture in the paper and knew you weren't.'

'Who says I don't have a tattoo?'

'I do.' He moved closer. 'And, as I've explored every centimetre of your body, I would know.'

She felt her face flood with colour.

'Do you know how pretty you look when you blush?' He stole another kiss, and another, and the next thing she knew they were lying on her sofa with one of his thighs thrust between hers, and his hands underneath the material of her strappy top.

'I think we're both a bit too old to do the teenage stuff,' she said. 'Seeing as I'm twenty-eight and I'm guessing that you're pushing thirty.'

'Over that particular hill already, I'm afraid. I'm thirty-four.'

'Well, you look good for your age, old man,' she teased.

He laughed. 'Keep insulting me, and I'm going to have to exact revenge. Which will involve you getting naked.'

'I do hope that's a promise. But maybe not on my sofa.'

'Time to be sensible?' He shifted to a sitting position.

'No, I just think somewhere more comfortable might be in order.'

'Are you propositioning me, Daisy Bell?'

She smiled. 'Yes.'

'Good.' He stood up and drew her to her feet. 'Take me to bed, Daisy.'

Daisy's bedroom wasn't quite what Felix had expected. It had cream walls, like the rest of the house, and a polished wooden floor with a bright rug on it. But it was dominated by the huge brass bed in the centre of the room. There was a patchwork throw across the quilt that he guessed was a family heirloom, and a pile of bright cushions that made him want to sink into them.

He turned to her. 'That's amazing,' he said softly. 'And I need you naked in that bed. Right now.'

'One moment.' She pulled the curtains, then sashayed back over to him, barefoot.

He pulled her to him and kissed her hard. She responded immediately, twining her fingers through his hair and pressing her body close to his.

He unbuttoned her jeans, enjoying the warmth and softness of her skin underneath his fingers. Then he peeled off her black strappy top and murmured in pleasure. 'I was hoping you'd be wearing a matching bra. I like this, Boots, I like it a lot.' He traced a path of kisses along the edge of her bra, then drew one nipple into his mouth, sucking it through the lace.

'Felix!' she gasped.

He stopped. 'OK?'

'Yes. *Very* OK.' Her voice had dropped an octave, telling him just how much she liked what he was doing to her. Good. He wanted her so turned on that she was incoherent.

He took it slowly, dropping to his knees in front of her and gradually stroking her jeans down over her hips, her thighs, her calves. He kissed the hollow of her ankles as he helped her step out of the denims, then the back of her knees, then a trail of kisses up her thighs, until she was quivering. When he slid one hand between her thighs, cupping her sex, he could feel the heat of her desire, how ready she was for him. He nuzzled her midriff, then gently drew her knickers down. 'Do you have any idea what you do to me, Daisy?'

'If it's like what you do to me, I think so.' Her voice was all breathy and husky, full of desire.

He pulled the covers back, picked her up and laid her against the pillows. He loved the way she looked, all soft and warm, her hair flowing over the pillows. 'You're incredible, Daisy,' he breathed, and stripped off his own clothes in a matter of seconds. He paused to put on a condom, and then he was right where he wanted to be: inside her, pushing deep, and watching the way her pupils went huge and her face went all drowsy with pleasure.

Then her body tightened round his, pushing him on to his own climax. He held her tightly, loving the feel of the aftershocks rippling through her body. Letting her go again was difficult, but he needed to deal with the condom.

'Bathroom?' he asked softly.

'Next door.'

When he came back, she'd curled up under the sheet. His cue to leave?

But then she lifted the sheet away from the other side of the mattress. 'Come back to bed,' she invited, and patted the mattress.

How could he resist?

He climbed into bed and gathered her into his arms. Daisy was easy to be with; he felt no pressure to make small talk. Lying there, listening to the evening birdsong with her in his arms, was all he wanted to do right now.

Not that he intended to stay with her tonight. Since

Tabitha, he'd avoided that kind of intimacy. Besides, this was meant to be a mad, crazy affair. One with strict limits.

And, however tempting he found Daisy, he wasn't going to break his rules.

CHAPTER TEN

OVER the next few weeks, they settled into a routine: Felix went back to London on Tuesday evenings and was back in Suffolk on Saturday morning, where he spent his days at the fairground and his evenings with Daisy.

Daisy found herself really enjoying Felix's company. She loved working with him, brainstorming ideas for promoting the fairground—everything from setting up educational days that fitted into the National Curriculum through to circus-skills training for kids and adults, with heritage events in between. At the weekends Felix helped her with some of the restoration work, wearing jeans and protective goggles and wielding a wire brush on the rusty patches of the chair-o-plane. It amazed her that he was prepared to go so far out of his natural environment, and it amazed her still further when it occurred to her that he was doing it for her.

In the middle of Tuesday evening, she was lying in Felix's arms in her big brass bed, sated from lovemaking, when he drew her closer. 'What are you doing on Saturday?'

'Working.' She frowned. He knew that. 'Why?'

'I was just wondering if you'd consider taking a day off.'

Her eyes narrowed. 'Are you nagging me, Mr Pot?'

He laughed and kissed her. 'No, Ms Kettle, because you could nag me right back. I just thought it might be nice to do something together.' He stole a kiss. 'Or, if you could manage a whole weekend, maybe you could come and stay with me in London.' Then he stopped. 'Sorry, I forgot, you can't. You're more than welcome to bring Titan with you, but he might not enjoy it in my flat.'

It warmed her that he'd thought of the cat's needs and that he recognised how much the ginger tom meant to her. 'You're right, he'd hate London.' She loved the fact that Felix had actually asked her to share his space, if only for a weekend. 'But I could get the train to London on Saturday morning, ask my neighbour to feed Titan on Saturday night and go home on Sunday morning.'

'*Late* Sunday morning,' he suggested. 'Make it a one-way ticket and I'll drive you home.'

'Felix, you don't have to do that.'

'I'm due back here anyway, so we might as well travel together.'

Oh. So he was being practical rather than sentimental. Well, of course he was. He'd asked her to spend time with him in London, but that didn't mean he was going to let her close. Or that he was going to declare his feelings for her. And she was wise enough to keep her own feelings to herself. Just so it didn't change things between them. 'OK.'

'Talk to Bill and let me know.' He kissed her again. 'I'd better be heading back to London, or it'll be stupid o'clock by the time I get home. I'll call you later.'

Bill actually sounded pleased that she wanted to take a couple of days off. And the anticipation of a snatched weekend with Felix helped to stop Daisy missing him over the next few days.

At last Saturday arrived. Daisy had given her spare key to her neighbour and arranged with her to feed Titan; she made a fuss of the cat before she left, and then at last she was on her way to Felix.

She loved the high, soaring arches and the ironwork of the station when she arrived at Liverpool Street; it was too long since she'd last visited London. Then she was past the ticket barrier and Felix was there, waiting for her. Two seconds later, she dropped her overnight bag and she was in his arms. He picked her up and swung her round, then kissed her lingeringly.

'Just as well they don't have a kissing ban at this station.'

He laughed. 'It wouldn't matter if they did. Nothing's going to stop me kissing my girl hello.'

My girl. The phrase made her feel warm all over. Was that how Felix saw her? Was he saying that he'd noticed the change in things between them, that it was more than an affair for him, too? Part of her wanted to ask, but another part of her couldn't face hearing the answer, just in case it wasn't the one she wanted. Or, worse, if it changed things between them: just as it had with her last three exes. They'd stopped seeing her for who she was, and had tried to change her into their ideal wife-to-be.

'I did think about driving you back to my place, but the traffic's hideous, so we're going by Tube.' He picked up her overnight bag. 'You travel light.'

'That's the good thing about not being girly. I don't

have to take six outfits and six pairs of shoes to choose from.'

He laughed. 'I've missed you, Boots.'

The admission made her chest feel tight. She'd missed him, too, more than she'd expected. And with every passing week she'd missed him more when he was away. Daily phone calls just weren't enough. 'Same here,' she said.

On the Tube, he pulled her onto his lap.

'Felix, we can't,' Daisy whispered, scandalised. 'Everyone's—'

He stopped her words with a brief kiss, then whispered in her ear. 'Nobody notices anyone on the Tube, and it's not as if I'm ripping your clothes off—even though I'm looking forward to doing that later. In private.'

The idea sent pleasure shivering through her, and she wrapped her arms round him. 'Sounds good to me,' she whispered back.

They changed onto the Docklands Light Railway; Felix's flat was only a few minutes' walk from the station. He let them both into the building, then ushered Daisy up to the penthouse.

'Your flat's enormous,' Daisy said, sounding shocked as she stood in the middle of his living room. 'This room alone is bigger than my entire ground floor.' She walked over to the window. 'And what an amazing view.' She took a deep breath. 'I didn't realise you were so wealthy.'

For a moment, Felix thought of Tabitha.

Then he pushed the paranoia away. Of course Daisy wasn't like his ex. She wasn't bothered about money—or she would've specialised in a different area of engineering, one that paid good rewards. She certainly wouldn't be working more than a full-time week in a museum for a part-time salary.

'I've just been lucky in my investments,' he said with a shrug. 'Can I get you something to drink?'

'I'm fine, thanks.' She looked slightly wary. 'So, what are the plans for tonight?'

He smiled at her. 'I thought we could go out for dinner and see a show.'

She bit her lip. 'Felix, that'd be lovely, but I wish you'd said earlier. I don't have any smart clothes with me.'

'No problem. It's already sorted.'

She frowned. 'How do you mean?'

He took her hand and led her into his guest bedroom. Hanging on the outside of the door, in a clear protective sleeve, was a dress he'd bought her the day before.

Her frown deepened. 'Felix, what is this?'

'A dress. For tonight.'

She looked straight at him. 'You bought me a dress,' she said slowly.

'And shoes. Yes.' This conversation really wasn't going the way it was supposed to go. Whenever he'd bought a dress for his sisters, they'd been delighted. Why was Daisy suddenly looking so upset?

'I think,' she said coolly, 'I might have made a mistake. I apologise for inconveniencing you, Felix. I'm going home.' She turned on her heel and walked out of the door.

He caught up with her in his living room. 'Daisy. What's wrong?'

'*You bought me a dress,*' she said through gritted teeth.

'What's the problem with that?'

She dragged in a breath. 'The problem is, you didn't ask me.'

'You hate the dress?' He was surprised, because he'd picked a classic shift dress in black slub silk. It was understated and yet feminine, like Daisy herself. He'd been pretty sure she'd like it, and that it would fit.

No matter.

'Fine. We'll go and change it.'

'It's not that.'

'Then what?'

She lifted her chin, and he was shocked to see tears in her eyes. 'I thought you were different.'

'Daisy, I'm really not following this.'

'It doesn't matter. I'm going home.'

'Not when you're this upset, you're not.' He wrapped his arms round her and held her close. 'Talk to me, Daisy. I can't read your mind. Just tell me what's so bad about a little black dress.'

She was shaking, and for a moment he thought that she was crying. Then she whispered, 'You're trying to change me. Just like they did.'

Who had tried to change her? But he focused on the first thing she'd said, his gut feeling telling him that this was the real reason why she was upset. He released his hold on her slightly so he could look into her face. 'Daisy, I'm not trying to change you. I like you as you are.'

She swallowed hard. 'But you want me to wear a dress. Which isn't me.'

'Actually, you looked lovely the last time I saw you wearing one,' he pointed out. 'I was just trying to do something nice for you and give you a special evening. I know you love musicals—you sing all the time at work—and I didn't tell you that I'd booked us tickets for a show because I wanted to surprise you. I thought you might enjoy glamming up for a night, and I know you don't usually wear dresses, so I bought one for you. Obviously I got it completely wrong. I'm sorry. I'll get rid of the dress, and if you don't mind me making a quick phone call I'll see if my PA would like the show tickets—it'd be a shame to waste them. And then you can tell me what you'd like to do tonight instead.'

It was what she wanted, wasn't it? So he'd expected her to look relieved. Instead, he saw the tears brim over her lashes and spill down her cheek. Silently, not with the dramatic kind of sobs Tabitha had indulged in. Whatever had upset her, it went bone-deep, and he ached for her.

He drew her closer again. 'Daisy, I'm sorry. I wouldn't have hurt you for the world.'

'No, I'm sorry. I'm so selfish,' she whispered.

'It's fine. And you're not. You're right: I *should* have asked you first.' Maybe she just didn't like surprises, which he could understand; he wasn't particularly keen on them, either. He much preferred being in charge of what was going on. He stroked her hair. 'Who tried to change you?' he asked softly.

'My ex.' She dragged in a breath. 'He was on the same course as me. We were eighteen when we started dating. And it was fine until he asked me to marry him.' She shivered. 'As soon as his ring was on my finger, he started to complain about the way I dressed, the way I did my hair, the fact I didn't wear much make-up. He had this idea of the perfect wife and he wanted me to fit it.'

Felix suddenly remembered the conversation he'd had with her about his type of woman. He'd realised back then that someone had put her down. What he hadn't guessed was just how badly. 'Daisy, your hair is glorious. There's nothing wrong with the way you dress.

And you don't need make-up—you're beautiful as you are. Your ex was incredibly stupid not to realise how lucky he was to have you, and I hope you made him eat his engagement ring.'

That earned him a watery smile. 'No, I just gave it back to him and told him I couldn't marry him.' She swallowed hard. 'But everyone I dated since…they were the same, too. Everything was fine until they were sure of me. Then they wanted to change me. I wasn't enough for them as I am.'

'I don't want to change you.' He stroked her face. 'All I wanted was to give you a special night out. No big deal, I promise.'

'I'm sorry. I overreacted.' She closed her eyes. 'I've made a real idiot of myself.'

'No, you haven't.' He risked stealing a kiss. 'Now you've told me, I can see exactly why you were upset. Give me a minute, and I'll offload the tickets.'

She bit her lip. 'Felix, can I be horribly greedy and contrary and say that actually I'd love to go to the show?'

'Just not in a dress?' he asked lightly.

She nodded. 'I'm sorry. It's a nice dress. And I know you went to a lot of trouble. Just…it's not who I am.'

'Despite having sisters, it's clear I don't understand women at all,' Felix said.

She swallowed hard. 'It's not you. It's me.' She sighed. 'Even my family complain that I'm not like other women.'

'Well, you're not. You're an individual,' he said, 'and that's not a criticism—it's part of your charm. Look, let's deal with your luggage. Then you can freshen up while I make us some coffee, and you can tell me where you fancy eating tonight before the show.' He released her and kissed the corner of her mouth. 'And I'll give you another choice, on the luggage front. You can stay in my guest suite, if you'd prefer, or in my room. It's up to you.' He paused. 'Though if you'd like to share my shower before we go out tonight, I promise not to complain.'

She brushed away another tear before it could fall. 'I really don't deserve you being so nice to me after I just had a huge tantrum on you. And I haven't said thank you for arranging tickets to a show.'

'Believe me,' he said dryly, 'that wasn't a huge tantrum.' It would have been barely a ripple for Tabitha.

She wrapped her arms round him. 'I'm sorry, Felix. I guess I'm a bit paranoid, after my ex.'

He could understand that; the same went for him. But he was dealing with it, trying to wipe Tabitha's words out of his head and out of his heart. 'Tell you what,' he said. 'How about a change of plan? Forget coffee and freshening up. I'm going to prove to you that I like you just as you are.'

And he did like her.

He more than liked her.

Not that he was ready to say so. Offering to spend the entire night with her was enough of a step for him right now. It was a lot more than he'd been prepared to offer anyone since Tabitha.

'Prove it? How?' she asked.

'Allow me to introduce you to Felix the Barbarian,' he said.

'Barbar—?'

Before she could finish the word, he picked her up and carried her into his bedroom, kicking the door closed behind him. 'Right. First of all, I'm going to take your clothes off. All of them. And then I'm going to explore every centimetre of your body with my hands and my mouth and tell you exactly how much you turn me on. I'm going to make you come at *least* twice.'

Her eyes darkened to jade as he set her on her feet again, letting her slide down his body so she was in no doubt about his arousal. 'Oh, really? Is that a promise, Mr Barbarian?'

'Yes.' He kissed her and gave her a lazy grin. 'And something you should know: I always keep my word.'

He did. To the point where they didn't actually have time for dinner before the show. It turned out that he'd booked tickets for one of Daisy's favourite musicals, *West Side Story*. As the first notes of 'Somewhere' spiralled through the theatre, Felix's fingers tightened round hers.

Could they find a place for each other? Daisy wondered.

He'd been so understanding about the dress, about the way she hated people trying to change her and make her feel that she didn't measure up. Felix saw her for who she was.

Maybe, just maybe, she was enough for him.

That was when she realised: their mad, crazy affair was nothing of the sort.

Not for her, at least. She'd fallen in love with an intense workaholic with a charming smile and a heart of pure gold. Though Felix would never admit to the latter, she knew. And he'd run a mile if he had any idea how she really felt about him—not to mention the fact that her last relationships had gone down the tubes as soon as the word 'love' had been spoken aloud. So she decided it was best to keep this particular revelation to herself, until she'd worked out how to deal with it.

She loved Felix.

And, although he'd refused to talk about it, she knew someone had hurt him in the past, too, to the point where he'd sworn off love and marriage. Whether he'd let her past his barriers, she really couldn't tell. Just hope.

After the show, they found a tiny bistro and Daisy insisted on picking up the bill. 'You bought the theatre tickets,' she said when Felix protested. And, just to make sure he wasn't difficult about it, she made the excuse that she needed to go to the toilet and paid the bill on her way from their table.

'Daisy, this was meant to be me treating you to a night out,' he said in exasperation when he found out what she'd done.

'You did. And what a night—the best seats in the house at my favourite musical.' She reached across the table and squeezed his hand briefly. 'Thank you.'

Felix hailed a taxi to take them back to Docklands, asking the cabbie to take the scenic route so they could see some of the most beautiful buildings in London lit up against the night.

Finally they wandered along the Thames towards his apartment block, arms wrapped round each other, watching the reflections of the lights on the water.

'Tonight has been amazing,' Daisy said softly.

'It hasn't finished yet.' He stole a kiss. 'Let's go home.'

Back at his flat, his lovemaking was slow and so tender that she almost cried. And she loved the way he curled protectively round her, drawing her back against his body as they slowly drifted into sleep. Right here, in his arms, she finally felt that she belonged. And maybe, just maybe, they had a future together.

CHAPTER ELEVEN

STAYING at Felix's marked a change in their relationship, because, when Daisy hesitantly suggested that Felix should stay at her place rather than in the hotel while he was in Suffolk, he actually agreed. He drove her crazy by tidying up, but he turned out to be a reasonable cook, taking another chore off her shoulders.

She'd never have guessed that such a hotshot businessman would have a domestic side, but she found it endearing. And she loved the fact that he didn't insist on traditional roles, the way her ex had.

Life was perfect—until one Wednesday morning when Nancy came in to the workshop.

Normally, Daisy would have been delighted to spend a while chatting with her aunt, but there were lines of strain etched into the older woman's face that worried her. She frowned. 'Nancy? Is something wrong?'

'Love, we need to talk.'

'Come and sit down.' Daisy found her a chair. 'Can I get you a coffee, a glass of water?'

'Nothing, thanks.' Nancy drew in a shuddering breath. 'It's Bill.'

Daisy went cold. 'What about him?'

'I made him go to the doctor's on Friday—and the doctor sent him for tests. We've got an appointment at the hospital next week.'

'What kind of tests?' Daisy asked.

'His heart.' Nancy bit her lip. 'The doctor says he needs to cut his hours down.'

'Down, or completely?' Daisy asked.

Nancy sighed. 'It depends what they find, but you know Bill. This place is his life. He's going to resist it.'

'I'll take as much pressure as I can off him. I'll put the restoration stuff on slow track and take over more of the paperwork.'

'I know you'll do your best, love. But you know Bill—he's still going to be worrying.'

'Then he'll need to come back to the fair just for fun, not to work, and leave me to make the decisions.' She gave her aunt her brightest smile. 'We all know I was going to take over from him, Nancy. It'll just be a bit sooner than any of us expected. Don't worry. I'll talk him round.'

Within a week, they knew for sure.

Bill had to retire, for the sake of his health.

'I can't dump all this on your shoulders,' Bill said. 'It's too much of a burden.'

'Of course it isn't,' Daisy said. 'I've been trained by the best. And you know I'll live up to your expectations—just as you did when you took over from Grandpa.'

'I don't know, Daisy.' His mouth compressed to a thin line. 'You're still young.'

'Not much younger than you were when you took over,' she pointed out. 'And being young also means that I have the stamina to deal with things.'

Bill shook his head. 'It's too much to ask.'

'I was really hoping you weren't going to make me play dirty,' she said. 'But you leave me no choice.'

His eyes narrowed. 'How do you mean?'

'Nancy and I, and the rest of the family, love you very, very much. We want you around for years and years to come. If you carry on as you are—' her voice wobbled and her eyes filled with tears as she thought about the scenario '—then we might only have you for a matter of months.' She gulped. 'And that's nowhere near long enough, Bill. Don't make us lose you. Nothing's worth that, even the fairground.'

He flinched. 'That's below the belt, Daze.'

'No, it's the truth.' She rubbed the tears away before they could fall. 'It's not too much to ask me to take over. But it *is* too much to make me watch you work yourself to death instead of letting me do something about it. Let me take over, Bill. If I hit problems, I'll talk to you about them. But, if you carry on as you are, your heart will give out and I'll have to take over in any case—except you won't be around to help me if I hit problems.'

She could see his eyes glittering with unshed tears. 'Daisy...'

'I'm so sorry.' She hugged him. 'You know I love you and I wouldn't hurt you for the world. But, if this is the only way to make you see reason, so be it. You'll still be chief trustee when we've finished sorting out the charity stuff. And I'll still be asking your opinion and listening to you. If I get the remotest sniff of a ghost train, I'm borrowing Ben's car and dragging you off to look at it to see what you think. But I want to take care of the stuff here, so you can take care of yourself.'

'Ned and Diana don't know how lucky they are,

having you,' Bill said, hugging her back. 'You're one in a million. The daughter Nancy and I wish I had.'

'Hey. You two are practically my second set of parents, and you know it.' Daisy swallowed the lump in her throat. 'So you're going to be reasonable about this?'

'I don't see that I have any choice.' Bill patted her shoulder. 'All right. On condition you talk to me about any problems.'

'Course I will.' She gave him her biggest, warmest smile.

She knew she wouldn't tell Bill about the big problem—the fact that taking over the complete running of the fairground meant that she'd have to find a mechanic to replace her, because there was no way she could do two full-time jobs at once, even if she worked crazier hours than she did now.

She really needed to talk to Felix.

She'd been through all the figures and she knew them off by heart. Right now, their finances couldn't stretch to paying someone else; just like Daisy, Bill didn't draw a full-time salary despite working more than full-time hours. What were the chances of finding a volunteer to work full-time for nothing? Practically zero. And, even when the charity paperwork was finally sorted out, any funding would pay for specific projects rather than for staff.

Felix had already talked an architect friend into designing a multi-purpose hall for them as a charitable donation, and had worked out a scheme where people could sponsor a brick to help with the building costs. He'd put his name down for an entire wall. She couldn't ask him for more.

Well, she could…but she was involved with him, and they'd agreed to keep their business and personal lives separate. Asking him for more cash to prop up her business was blurring the line way too much, in her view. But she *could* ask his advice, ask him to brainstorm things with her and help her work out a killer sponsorship deal that would tempt someone else to invest in a different area of the fairground.

It was the kind of thing they'd need to do face to face rather than on the phone. So she'd ask him on Saturday, when they planned a snatched weekend together. Steal a little bit of their personal time for business. Felix would understand, she was sure.

On Saturday morning, Felix was stocking up on Daisy's favourite nibbles in the supermarket when a trolley collided with his.

He looked up automatically—and wished he hadn't.

'Felix! Hello.' The petite, well-groomed brunette looked absolutely thrilled to see him.

He didn't feel thrilled to see her. Far from it. Since he'd walked out, all communications had been via his solicitor. This was the first time he'd seen her in three years, and he was shocked to realise that it still hurt. He certainly didn't love her any more, and he didn't want her back in his life, but seeing her reminded him of why he'd walked out. How she'd taken his heart and stomped over it. 'Tabitha,' he responded coolly.

'It's so good to see you, Felix.'

He gave her a forced and very polite smile.

'You're looking well,' she said, giving him her brightest smile in return. The kind of smile she used to give him before cosying up to him—and then she'd mention that she'd seen something just *darling* in a shop and it would go so nicely with her dress or her favourite shoes. With a price tag to match.

His gaze went automatically to her left hand. She was sporting an enormous diamond on her ring finger, larger even than the one he'd bought her. Maybe her new partner had enough money to keep her happy and it didn't bother him if he wasn't loved, the way it had bothered Felix. 'You look well, too.' Pampered. Just as she'd wanted to be.

Just as she had been, when she'd been engaged to him.

'So, what are you doing here?' she asked.

He indicated his basket. 'Shopping.' He almost added, 'buying treats for my girlfriend', but that sounded too defensive. And he didn't want Tabitha thinking she'd rattled him. 'You?' And please, please don't say you've moved from our old flat and have become a near neighbour, he begged silently. He really didn't want to keep bumping into her, raking up the old hurt over and over again.

She shrugged. 'Just getting a few things for a girly night in.'

Several bottles of wine, low-calorie dips and ready-prepared crudités.

Yeah. He remembered her girly nights in.

More than that, he remembered *that* conversation on their balcony. And the knife that had twisted in his heart when he'd overheard it.

From the colour staining her cheeks, so did she.

It wasn't the kind of thing you could forget. Felix hadn't forgiven it, either. It was a truism that eavesdroppers heard no good of themselves, but he hadn't intended to eavesdrop. Though he was relieved that he'd heard her and discovered how she'd really felt before it was too late. Her self-justification and panic, once she'd realised that she'd lost her golden goose, had sickened him.

'I'd better let you get on,' she said, fluttering her lashes at him. 'But maybe we could do lunch some time. Catch up on things.'

This was surreal. And certainly a lot more polite than their last conversation. Maybe that was it: she was just trying to be polite, and the offer meant nothing.

But then she added, 'It'd be *so* good to see you, Felix,' and placed her hand on his arm in the old familiar way.

What? He could hardly believe what he was hearing. This was the woman who'd taken him to the cleaners. Did she seriously think he'd want to hook up with her again in *any* kind of capacity?

Then again, he'd let himself be blind to her faults first time round. As their relationship had developed, his judgement had gone out of the window, and he'd let her reel him in. All the way. Now, here he was, squeezing time out of his crazy schedule to find Daisy's favourite treats.

He'd really learned nothing about relationships, had he?

'I'd better get on,' he said coolly.

He went straight to the checkout, regardless of the fact that he hadn't quite finished. The idea of bumping into Tabitha in every single aisle really didn't appeal.

He was still edgy when he met Daisy at the station. She was quiet, too; no doubt his mood had communicated itself to her. He was annoyed with himself for spoiling the weekend—it wasn't as if they managed to get much time off together—but he just couldn't shift the resentment that seemed to bubble through his veins.

Still, back at his flat, he made the effort. 'Are you OK? You're a bit quiet.'

She bit her lip. 'Felix, I hate to ask…'

Another voice echoed in his head: *Felix, I hate to ask, but I'm a bit short this month.* Because Tabitha had spent all her salary on clothes—clothes she'd claimed to need to wear out to functions with him. He hadn't seen why she couldn't wear the same dress more than once, but she'd insisted otherwise.

'What?' he asked, aware that his tone was sharp.

She shook her head. 'Never mind.'

But then she went quiet on him.

He could remember Tabitha doing that, too, if he'd been offhand with her when she'd interrupted him while he was concentrating on a set of figures. And it had always cost him afterwards—an expensive floral apology, dinner out, jewellery of some description. He ground his teeth.

'Why don't you save us both the time and spit it out?'

She looked at him as if he'd grown two heads. 'Felix, what's wrong?'

'Nothing.'

She raised an eyebrow. 'You don't usually growl at people for nothing.'

'I'm not growling.'

'No?' She lifted her chin. 'Look, Felix, if you're not going to talk to me about whatever the problem is, and you're going to be in this mood all weekend, I might as well go home, because this isn't going to work.'

Tell her. Just tell her about Tabitha. Tell her that you saw your ex today and it's rattled you.

But he couldn't. Couldn't be that weak. Couldn't admit that he'd tried for the last three years to get past the fear that women saw him only in terms of what he could give them—and that even now there was a part of him that wondered if Daisy saw him for himself or for what he could give her business. Even though intellectually he knew he was being unfair to her, insulting her, he couldn't shift the fear from his heart.

And he hated himself for it.

He closed his eyes. 'I apologise for being grumpy. Don't go.'

She stroked his face. 'OK. If you're sure you want me to stay. But I'm worried about you, Felix. I think you're working too hard.'

Another of Tabitha's favourite comments, usually followed by a complaint that he was neglecting her.

Oh, for pity's sake. He had to *stop* this. If anything, Daisy was more of a workaholic than he was. She rarely took any time off—today was a snatched day.

'I'm fine,' he said.

Her expression said she didn't believe a word, but to his relief she didn't push him. How could he explain what was in his head?

But Daisy was quiet all afternoon, not like her usual self at all.

He knew it was his fault. Eventually, he sighed. 'I'm sorry I'm being difficult.'

'It's OK. I'm not great company right now, either. I haven't been sleeping well.'

The admission surprised him but, now he looked at her, he could see shadows under her eyes. 'What's wrong?'

'We're not getting as many people as I'd hoped buying a brick to help build the hall.' She bit her lip. 'The way things are going, we're going to need a lot more investment in the fairground. And not just for building work.'

Meaning that she expected *him* to invest?

Felix was taken right back to the moment when he'd walked into his flat and heard Tabitha and her friends talking on the balcony.

'Of course I don't love Felix—but I do love the life-style he gives me.'

'*He's pretty easy on the eye, Tab.*'

'*Oh, yes, I don't deny he's nice looking.*' A tinkling laugh. '*But he's so dull!*'

Tabitha had taken everything he'd given her and still asked for more, and it looked as if Daisy intended to do the same. He'd already agreed to a big sponsorship deal with the fairground, but it clearly wasn't enough for her.

After all he'd promised himself, it seemed he'd made the same mistake all over again: he'd let himself fall for a woman who saw him for his bank account instead of for himself. He'd thought that Daisy was different, that what they shared was special. He'd let himself fall in love with her, let himself believe that she was falling for him. And all along she'd seen him as someone who could prop up her failing business.

How stupid could he get?

So much for once bitten, twice shy. He might just as well have been carrying a placard saying, 'I'm rich and I'm a sucker for a pretty face and a sob story. Come and fleece me'.

Pain made him sharp. 'So you're hoping that the bank of Felix Gisbourne will sort out the fairground, hmm?'

She stared at him in apparent shock.

Ha. As well she might. He had her measure now.

And then her lip curled. 'Forget I said anything.'

Too late. She'd already said it.

'And you know what? I think it's time to call a halt. To everything.' She lifted her chin. 'It's just as well we haven't started building work on the hall. I wasn't asking you for money, Felix.' Her eyes were filled with disgust. 'You can keep your precious money. Send me an invoice for the time you've spent at the fairground. And I don't ever want to see you again.'

'Good. Because I never want to see you again, either.'
And he'd never, ever trust another woman for as long
as he lived.

In answer, she slammed his front door. Hard.

And Felix had to stifle his urge to smash every piece
of glass in the place.

Daisy caught the first train back to Suffolk, shocked
beyond belief.

Her entire life appeared to be sliding into an abyss.
The man she loved had just accused her of expecting
him to prop up her business, when she hadn't asked him
anything of the kind; she'd been trying to tell him about
Bill and the problems they were facing.

And he'd said he never wanted to see her again.

So much for thinking he might be falling for her. He
was cold, unfeeling—*impossible*. How could she have
been so stupid?

And everything was going wrong at the fairground.
The estate agent she'd seen the day before, when she'd
been hoping that she could raise some cash by selling her
house, had warned her that in the current market she'd
have to take a big drop in the asking price to get a quick
sale. Given that she already had a loan to pay back for
the plate-glass windows and would need to keep some
of the proceeds of the sale to rent a small flat somewhere,
she knew that if she sold the house at a knock-down price
she wouldn't have enough to plug the hole in the fairground's finances for more than a few months.

And, with Bill retiring, she'd be stuck doing admin
instead of the job she loved so much.

Life sucked.

Big time.

As soon as Daisy was back home, she changed back into her jeans and an old T-shirt and cycled over to the fairground, but her workshop didn't seem to hold its usual magic. She couldn't concentrate on what she was doing; all she could hear was Felix's voice echoing in her head. *I never want to see you again, either.*

She stayed working until long after everyone else had gone, but her mood wouldn't lift. She didn't want to dump her problems on Ben and Alexis, and as it was a Saturday night Annie would no doubt be out somewhere with her fiancé. It wasn't fair to dump things on her, either.

'Looks like it's just you and me, Titan,' she told the cat.

But even curling up on the sofa with him, a tub of ice-cream and one of her favourite musicals didn't help. She couldn't stop thinking about Felix, remembering how it had been between them—and then seeing the rejection on his face when he'd told her that he never wanted to see her again.

How had it all gone so badly wrong? Everything had vanished in a matter of seconds.

Well, now she knew for sure that she wasn't cut out for relationships. And she was never, *ever* going to let herself fall in love with anyone again.

Just over a week later, Felix reached the last item of his post: his regular report from the cuttings agency containing articles clipped from newspapers over the past month about projects he'd been involved with during the last year.

He flicked through it. The second he saw Daisy's picture, he closed the file and shoved it in a drawer without reading it.

He really didn't want to think about Daisy. He'd just

started to trust again, to think that maybe it was possible she'd want to be with him for his own sake, not because of his bank account—and she'd shattered his trust. It hurt far more than Tabitha's betrayal because he'd really believed that Daisy was different.

But the article nagged at him.

All morning.

And mid-afternoon he finally gave in, fished the file out of the drawer and turned to the page that had stopped him in his tracks.

The article was written by Annie Sylvester, Features Editor—the one who'd written the original article about the vandalism. Daisy's best friend:

END OF AN ERA

What?

He glanced at the date. It had been written three days ago.

Frowning, he skimmed through the piece. And when he reached the end he was stunned. Bill was retiring through ill health, and the Bells were selling the fairground at the end of the season.

It didn't make sense. Daisy loved that fairground more than anything else. She'd taken out a loan on her house to pay for the café windows, and she was capable of selling every single one of her personal possessions if she thought it would save the fairground.

Why were they selling up? Why hadn't she asked him to help her broker some kind of deal to save the fairground?

And then it hit him.

She had asked him—or she'd tried to, at least. That

weekend when he'd been in a foul temper after bumping into Tabitha.

Felix, I hate to ask...

She'd used a trigger phrase that had immediately put him on the defensive. The phrase he'd always associated with a request for money, thanks to his ex.

We're going to need a lot more investment.

He'd jumped straight to the conclusion that she wanted his money. But had she really?

You can keep your precious money. Send me an invoice for the time you've spent at the fairground.

She hadn't actually asked him to make the investment himself. Now he'd cooled down and could look at it dispassionately, he realised she'd included him in the 'we', as part of the fairground management team. So she'd obviously wanted to discuss it with him, talk about the impact of Bill's retirement on the business and the best way to deal with it.

And he'd been so full of resentment and anger from seeing Tabitha that morning he'd gone off at the deep end, not seeing what was right in front of his nose. He'd made the biggest mistake of his life, a far bigger error than trusting Tabitha.

He hadn't trusted Daisy.

How could he have been so stupid? This was the woman who'd insisted on buying him dinner because he'd bought the theatre tickets and she wanted to pay her way. She certainly wouldn't have seen him as the trophy husband who would give her a generous allowance as well as picking up the tab for designer clothes and shoes, an exclusive gym membership and an account at her favourite beauty salon, the way Tabitha had. Apart from the fact that Daisy would be bored stiff by the lifestyle of a lady who lunched, she was proud. Independent. She'd reacted really badly when he'd just bought her a dress.

He'd seen something in her that simply wasn't there. He'd judged her by the standards of his ex and the kind of women that his well-meaning but clueless mother kept trying to fix him up with.

He needed to see her. To apologise face to face.

And he knew exactly where he was going to find her.

CHAPTER TWELVE

THE rush-hour traffic was ridiculous, and it was well past closing time when Felix parked at the fairground. Though he knew Daisy was still there, because he could see the light glimmering through her office window.

The gate was locked, but he still had the key Bill had given him. A key he should really have returned a week ago, but he'd blocked out the fact that he still had it. It took a matter of seconds to unlock the gate and secure it again behind him.

He couldn't hear her singing as he drew nearer. Well, she wouldn't be, would she? She was stuck in the office instead of in the workshop she loved.

Maybe he could do something about that.

He stood in the doorway for a moment, watching her as she worked. The shadows under her eyes had deepened, and she'd lost weight. Right at that moment, she looked vulnerable. Fragile. His heart ached for her; she was carrying such a burden. And, when she'd come to him for help, he'd pushed her away and hurt her.

Quietly, he rapped on the door.

She glanced up and he could see the shock on her face. 'What are you doing here?' she asked.

'I've come to apologise.'

Her lip curled. 'Don't bother. And you know the way out.'

'I've come to apologise,' he said again, walking in and sitting on the chair opposite her desk, ignoring the fact that she'd told him to go. 'To explain. And to listen.'

'I'm not interested.'

'If you keep hitting keys at random, eventually you're going to delete stuff you actually need,' he pointed out softly. 'Daisy, I'm sorry. I was completely in the wrong. I didn't listen to you or give you a chance to tell me about Bill. I let other stuff get in the way, and I accused you of something I know you'd never do. I know I don't have the right to ask this, but…' He took a deep breath. 'Will you let me explain?'

She looked at him for a long moment. Finally she nodded.

Getting her to agree to listen had been the easy part. Now he had to talk. Say the words he'd never told anyone else, even his family.

'I was…involved with someone,' he said. 'It didn't end well. I bumped into her the morning you came to London, and I guess it rattled me. So I wasn't in the mood to listen when you tried to tell me what was going on at the fairground.'

'And that's it?' Daisy folded her arms. 'That's your explanation? You'd seen someone who rattled your cage, so you took it out on me?'

'It's not quite like that.' He knew it wasn't enough of an explanation. He was going to have to tell her the rest of it.

How he hated saying it out loud. It was like pressing on a bruise that went all the way through him. But if he was ever to have a chance of working things out with Daisy he was going to have to talk to her. 'I came home early one day, planning to surprise her. She was on the balcony.'

Daisy's face was so open; he could see the conclusion she'd jumped to. 'She wasn't alone,' he confirmed. 'But it wasn't what you're thinking. She wasn't with a lover.' Maybe he would've found it easier to deal with if she had been. At least then he'd have known that it was love and passion that had driven Tabitha, not sheer, calculating, mercenary greed. He could've understood that. Forgiven it.

'What then?' Daisy asked.

'She was talking to her friends. None of them heard me come in, so they didn't stop talking or change the topic. And that's when I found out how she really felt about me.'

More pressure on the bruise.

He looked away, unable to face the pity he knew he'd see in Daisy's eyes as he said the words he'd kept locked inside for so long. 'She said she didn't love me, but she loved the lifestyle I could give her. I was nice looking, she said, but I was oh, so *dull*.'

'She said *what*?'

'She didn't want me for me,' Felix said, saying it out loud for the first time. 'She wanted me for what I could give her.'

'That's…' Daisy shook her head. 'I don't know what to say. I can't understand how anyone could think like that.'

Neither could he. But it had made him doubt everything: his family, his friends, and later girlfriends. Catastrophically, it had made him doubt Daisy. 'When you started talking to me that day,' he said, 'you used a few of the phrases I associate with her.'

The outrage and shock on Daisy's face grew deeper. 'You thought I was like *her*? That I was only with you because of your money?'

He closed his eyes. 'I told you I owed you an apology. A big one.'

'What she did to you was cruel and unfair, and I'm sorry she hurt you like that, but how…?' She shook her head, her eyes sparking with anger. 'How could you possibly think I was like that, Felix? You *know* I'm not. Money isn't important to me. For pity's sake, I don't even take a full-time salary from the fairground!'

'When I'm thinking straight, of course I know that. I wasn't thinking straight that day.' He moistened his suddenly dry lips. 'I heard you speak, but she was in my head, and I jumped to the wrong conclusion.' Though, to be fair, he wasn't the only one who'd behaved that way. 'Just as you did when I bought you that dress and you accused me of wanting to change you, the way your ex had.'

She folded her arms. 'So that's it? You were getting revenge on me?'

'No. Nothing like that at all. What I'm saying is that when an idea's stuck in your head it can stop you from seeing things how they really are. What happened with Tabitha made me doubt a lot of things. Even my family.'

'I can see now why you see marriage as a trap, when yours ended up like that,' Daisy said thoughtfully.

'We weren't married. Not quite,' he amended.

Daisy frowned. 'I'm not with you.'

'The wedding was booked for that weekend.' He paused. 'I called it off and told everyone I had cold feet.'

'Hang on. She was the one in the wrong, but you took the blame?'

He shrugged. 'I was the one who walked out.'

'With good reason.'

'It was that or let the whole world know the woman I planned to marry only saw me in terms of my bank account and thought that I was dull,' he said dryly. 'And I was a teensy bit too proud to play the victim.' He looked away. 'I'm just glad I overheard that conversation when I did, and not a week after the honeymoon. It saved a legal mess.'

'Felix, that's so…' Her words tailed off.

'I'd rather you didn't pity me, thank you.'

'I don't pity you. But you didn't deserve to be treated that way.' She blew out a breath. 'Now I know why you went all arctic on me when I teased you about all work and no play that time. You thought I was calling you dull.'

Just as his ex-fiancée had done.

He remained silent.

'You're not dull, Felix. Not in the slightest. Surely you must know that?'

'Considering the way your ex treated you made you believe that you're not feminine enough,' he said, 'are you telling me that you realise now you're all woman?'

She was silent for a long time. 'No,' she admitted eventually. 'I'm paranoid. Like you. You're right—the memories do get in the way sometimes.' She shook her head. 'So you haven't told anyone the truth about what happened? How could you let them blame you?'

He shrugged. 'I'd rather people think me cold than an easy target.'

'There's nothing easy about you, Felix,' she said dryly.

'That's what my family said.' He dragged in a breath. 'And Tabitha made me doubt them, too. I looked back at my childhood with new eyes.'

'How do you mean?'

'Remember when you asked if I had a lonely childhood? You were right, I did, because I was away at boarding school and my sisters went to school locally. And after Tabitha…'

'You thought your parents sent you away because you weren't interesting enough, because they didn't love you?'

She'd said the words he couldn't bring himself to say, and it felt like wire wool scrubbing at his heart. 'It happens,' he said tonelessly.

'You also once told me your family's big on tradition. Did your father go to the same school by any chance?'

'Yes. And my grandfather.'

'That's the real answer, Felix. They were doing things the way they'd always been done, instead of seeing that maybe their son needed something different.'

'Maybe.'

'Ask them,' Daisy said. There was a long silence, and then she asked softly, 'Are you still in love with her?'

'No. I was in love with a woman that I thought loved me all the way back. It turned out that wasn't who she was. I'm over it now.'

Her expression called him a liar.

'I don't love her.' Because he was in love with Daisy. But he'd hurt her so badly that he wasn't sure she could ever bring herself to love him. There was one thing he could do for her, though: fix the fairground's finances and make her life easier. 'So, now we've got that out of the way, we need to talk about the fairground. So what's this about Bill?'

'Heart condition. He needs to retire, for his health's sake.'

'Which makes you the manager?'

She nodded.

'With no time for your restoration work and the stuff you love doing. Not to mention the fact that you need to pay someone else to take your place. You're short of money. Well, I can sort that for you.'

She folded her arms. 'I don't want your money, Felix.' Her voice was very cool, very precise. 'Get that straight. Not everyone sees people in terms of what they can get out of them. And you haven't sent me that invoice yet.'

'What invoice?'

'For the time you've spent on the fairground. Consultancy fee, remember?'

He rolled his eyes. 'I'm not going to send you an invoice. Not now, not ever. Daisy, you can't afford to pay me.'

'Yes, I can.' She gave him a stubborn glare. 'I'll find the money somewhere. I'm not accepting your charity.'

He sighed. 'So your solution is to put the fairground up for sale—when it's the love of your life.'

She shrugged. 'Didn't work out. Guess that's the story of my love life. Time to move on.'

'To what? Work as a more conventional mechanic and be miserable? Surely you'd rather be here?'

Her eyes glittered. 'Don't rub it in.'

'I'm not. I'm saying that I can fix this for you and I want to help.'

She shook her head. 'You seriously think I'm going to work with you again, after what happened between us?'

'I know I'm asking a lot here, but I think we can make this work together.'

She was silent, and he began to hope.

Then she lifted her chin. 'Strictly business. Nothing personal.'

'A business partnership,' Felix said. 'Forget about sponsorship deals. The fairground's up for sale.'

'And you're offering to buy it?'

'Part of it,' he said. 'Which should free up enough funds to employ a full-time office manager, and take the stuff you hate off your shoulders so you can go back to doing what you love instead of feeling trapped in the office. You'll still be in charge, but you don't have to do the grinding stuff.'

'What happens when you decide you've had enough and want to sell your share?'

'That's not going to happen.'

Her eyes narrowed. 'How can you be so sure?'

'Because someone once told me,' he said softly, 'that seeing the good in things is a lot healthier than being cynical and believing that everyone's out solely for what they can get.'

'But your experience told you that...' Her voice tailed off.

'That Tabitha was out solely for what she could get,' he finished. 'But not everyone's like her. You're definitely not. And I'm sorry I hurt you, Daisy.'

She dragged in a breath. 'I can understand why you acted the way you did. But it's business only between us from now on. I can't deal with anything else.'

It wasn't what he'd wanted her to say.

But it was better than having her out of his life completely. 'OK,' he said. 'I'll talk to Bill tomorrow.'

'No. I don't want him stressed.'

'So the deal's between you, me and the lawyers?'

'And when we've come to an agreement *then* we'll talk to Bill,' she said. 'Not before.'

He looked at her. 'When did you last eat?'

She shrugged. 'I'll eat when I get home. With Titan.'

In other words, she didn't want to eat with him.

'Can I at least give you a lift home?' he asked.

'No.'

Pushing her now would be the wrong thing to do, Felix knew. It would just deepen the rift between them. 'Then perhaps we can meet tomorrow at ten, for preliminary discussions?'

'Sure. You know where to find me.'

Over the next fortnight, Felix worked with Daisy. He kept it strictly business between them, as she'd asked: official meetings, the occasional email with suggestions and attached legal documents. Though when he did see her he ached to touch her. To wrap his arms round her and tell her that everything was going to be fine from now on, because he'd support her and he'd never let her down again. Because he loved her more than he'd ever loved anyone in his entire life.

But he knew he was going to have to take this at Daisy's pace, give her time to learn to trust him again. And then, please God, she might let him back into her life the way she had before. Give him a second chance.

Strictly business. It had been Daisy's own suggestion. How did the old saying go? *Be careful what you wish for. You might get it.*

She'd got it, all right.

And it wasn't what she wanted.

Meetings with Felix were getting harder and harder. He was perfectly polite to her, and always talked business to her, but she wanted their old relationship back. The one where he called her by that ridiculous nickname and stole kisses and challenged her.

Most of all, she wanted to fall asleep in his arms. Maybe then she wouldn't wake up at stupid o'clock, worrying about the future, because she had him by her side and they'd get each other through it.

Sometimes she caught an expression in his eyes, but it was always so fleeting that she thought she'd imagined it. Had seen what she wanted to see.

Love.

But Felix didn't love her. After the way his ex had hurt him, she wasn't sure he'd ever be able to love again. So it was pointless wishing for something she'd never be able to have.

The day that Felix and Daisy signed the contract making him a partner in the fairground, they shook hands on the deal. It was the first time he'd touched her for weeks, and it made him want more. Even though it was merely a polite business handshake, it sent ripples of desire all the way through him.

He couldn't help catching her eye, and she was definitely looking at his mouth. He watched colour bloom in her cheeks as she glanced up and realised he'd caught her. And then, very deliberately, he looked at her mouth before glancing up again to meet her gaze.

Felix had a feeling that they were thinking the same way: maybe they should seal the deal properly. With a kiss.

And how he wanted to kiss her. How he wanted her

to kiss him back, slide her arms round his neck and press her body against his. How he wanted to peel her clothes off and lose himself in her.

Maybe, Felix thought, it was time to take a risk.

CHAPTER THIRTEEN

LATE that evening, Daisy had just made herself a mug of tea and flopped in a chair in the kitchen when her doorbell rang.

She wasn't expecting visitors. Maybe it was Annie or Alexis, bearing chocolate and intending to nag her about letting up the pace a bit. She psyched herself up to smile brightly, then headed for the door.

When she opened it, she blinked in surprised. 'Felix.'

He was the last person she'd expected. She'd told him it was strictly business between them.

Then again, he'd caught her staring at his mouth this morning, remembering what it was like to kiss him and wishing things were different.

'Hello, Daisy. May I come in?'

No. Not if she was to have a hope in hell of keeping him at a distance in future.

'I need to talk to you about something,' he said softly. 'Something important.'

His face was utterly sincere. And there were shadows beneath his eyes that told her he'd been having trouble sleeping, too. Maybe the situation was as tough for him as it was for her. Not that she dared let herself hope.

'OK,' she said finally.

'I just need to get something from the car,' he said.

Oh. Paperwork. Well, of course he'd only be here for business purposes. 'Sure. I'm in the kitchen. Do you want a cup of tea?'

'No. But thank you for asking.'

How had they become reduced to this distant politeness? Then again, she'd been the one who'd insisted on the terms: work, and nothing else. It was her own fault.

When Felix came into the kitchen, he was carrying a large, deep cardboard box.

'What's that?' she asked.

'Props.'

'Props? What kind of props?' She wasn't following a word of this. Or maybe she'd fallen asleep at her kitchen table and was having some kind of surreal and very realistic dream. When she woke, she'd be alone, and there was so much distance between herself and Felix, he might as well be on the other side of the world.

She pinched herself surreptitiously. It hurt. So he really was here.

What she didn't understand was why.

He set the box at the far end of her kitchen table. 'I'm giving you a biology lesson.'

Daisy thought of his naked body and blushed to the roots of her hair.

'About plants. Botany,' he corrected himself hastily.

'I don't need a botany lesson.'

'Yes, you do. We both do.' He paused. 'I'm going to tell you about daisies. There are lots of different kinds of daisy. And each one is like a different part of you.'

He reached into the box and brought out a pot. 'This is the English daisy, *Bellis perennis*. The name's from the Saxon, meaning "day's eye", because it opens in the morning, follows the sun and closes at night. And that's you, Daisy. A wild flower, bright as the day.'

His words made her speechless.

He handed her the pot before taking another one from the box. 'And this is a gerbera, a different sort of daisy. Very sturdy. This is you at work, solid and dependable. Though it's also vibrant, like you. Strong.' He handed her the pot.

Daisy couldn't quite work out where he was taking this. But it was clear he'd put a lot of thought into it and that he was absolutely sincere. His eyes were a deep, dark grey, and although he'd adopted a relaxed air she could almost feel the tension humming through his body. The same tension that was humming through hers.

Could he…?

'And this,' he said, taking out yet another pot, 'is a rain daisy, *Dimorphotheca pluvialis*. It likes the sun and it closes if it's going to rain. A bit like you, closing up when you're taken away from the fairground.'

Her throat closed. Oh God, no. She was reading this completely wrong. She'd started to hope that he was telling her how he felt, but now she went cold. Was he telling her…? She had to know. 'You're taking the fairground from me?' she whispered.

'I went into partnership with you today, Daisy,' he reminded her. 'To make sure the fairground can't be taken from you.'

'So why are you doing this, Felix? Why are you showing me all these flowers?'

'Because I want you to know something. There are

lots of different daisies. Sturdy ones, sensitive ones, wild ones and sexy ones. And all of them are *you*.'

'*Sexy?*' She was completely baffled. 'How can a flower possibly be sexy?'

He produced another pot from his box. '*Argyrantheum*, or the Paris daisy. I know pink isn't usually your colour, but bear with me. It's spiky outside, with the leaves like a star. And inside it's lush and beautiful, just like you. Sexy as hell. If this flower was human, it'd look like you do when you've been thoroughly kissed all over.'

She dragged in a breath. She knew precisely how many minutes it was since she'd last been in his arms. Since he'd last kissed her. Since he'd teased her with his mouth before easing into her body.

Right now, he was making love to her again. With words and flowers.

Not just any flowers, either: daisies. Flowers that made him think of her.

And he was telling her exactly how he felt about her. At last, he was opening his heart to her.

'I wanted to get you some blue Michaelmas daisies, but apparently they flower in September, so that was a no-no. This is the best I could do.' He handed her a piece of paper with a picture of a Michaelmas daisy. 'But you don't expect to find a blue daisy. It's unusual. Like you. And, just in case you're thinking what I think you're thinking, that's unusual in a *good* way.'

She wanted to cry. Weep. Beg him to stop if he didn't mean it. Because right now her heart was cracking wide open.

He produced another pot. 'This is *Leucanthemum vulgare*, the ox-eye daisy. Sometimes it's called the moon daisy or the dog daisy—in France they call it "Marguerite".' He held her gaze. 'And they're the ones that are supposed to be used for "he loves me, he loves me not". Care to try it?'

She hardly dared believe him. 'You're not in love with me, Felix.'

'Are you sure about that?' He raised an eyebrow. 'I dare you to find out.'

She wrapped her arms round herself, shivering. 'Why are you doing this?'

'Because,' he said, 'I think we both feel the same way. And we're both scared to admit it, because people have hurt us in the past and we've hurt each other, and neither of us wants to risk it happening again. But, if we're to have a chance, one of us has to take a risk and be the first to say it. So I'm being brave. I'm telling you what I see in you.'

All the different types of daisies. Did he really think there were so many facets to her? Shy and sensitive; solid and dependable; strong and vibrant; spiky; lush and sexy.

'I dare you,' he said again, his voice very soft.

She picked a single ox-eye daisy from the pot and took the petals off, one at a time. 'He loves me, he loves me not…'

There were twenty-one white petals.

He loves me.

'I was the one who pushed you away,' he said quietly. 'And it's the biggest mistake I ever made. If it takes me the rest of my life to make it up to you, Daisy, I'll do it. Because I love you and I want a proper relationship with you. Not just business. Not seeing each other in secret and hiding away from everyone. I want to be with you and I want the whole world to know that I'm yours and you're mine.'

Two seconds later, she was in his arms. 'Felix. I never thought I'd ever hear you say that. And I love you, too. These last few weeks…'

'It's felt as if there wasn't any sunshine left in the world,' Felix said.

'Same for me,' she whispered.

His kiss was sweet, gentle at first, and then became more demanding as she responded to him. By the time he broke the kiss, they were both breathless and her pulse was hammering.

'I love you, Daisy. I know we're both going to have to make compromises—I need to move my business here from London, and we're going to have to get a bigger house. But we'll work it out between us, because we'll talk to each other. No clamming up. Because I'm on your side, and I want you on mine.'

'Snap,' Daisy said.

He kissed her again. 'There is one last daisy,' he said. 'And you need to see this one.' He handed her a retro-style toy: a daisy in a bright-orange pot wearing sunglasses. He whistled 'Just The Way You Are' and the flower started to dance.

She burst out laughing. 'Felix, that's…' She shook her head, still smiling, unable to think of a suitable comment.

'Seemed appropriate, with you singing all the time. And the song's important, too. I'll take issue with the "clever conversation" bit because I enjoy sparring with you, but the rest of it's true. I love you as you are. I don't want you to change. And, Daisy, I believe in you.'

'I believe in you, too,' she said softly.

He stroked her face. 'There was one other thing.'

'What?'

'You and I—we've been here before. I proposed to

someone, and you accepted a proposal. And they both went wrong. But I'm not your ex, just as you're not Tabitha. I know you don't want me for my money.' His grey eyes were intense. 'And I hope you know I love you for yourself. You make my world a better place.' He dragged in a breath. 'Maybe I should've planned this better. I should've taken you out to dinner, walked with you on a beach in the moonlight and asked you there. But I don't want to wait. I don't want to be without you any longer.' He dropped to one knee. 'Daisy Bell, will you do me the honour of marrying me? Will you be the love of my life, and never, ever change?'

And through her tears she heard herself whisper, 'Yes.'

EPILOGUE

Two months later

FELIX stepped out of the car and walked through the lych gate. His parents, Daisy's mother and brothers, Bill and Nancy were waiting by the church door.

His mother greeted him with a hug. 'You look wonderful, darling. But nervous.'

So nervous that he hadn't been able to eat breakfast. Or lunch. But he forced a smile to his face. 'Are you kidding? This is going to be the best day of my life, the start of my future.' He took a tiny hand-cranked musical box from his pocket and turned the handle; the first few bars of 'Get Me To The Church On Time' tinkled into the air.

Bill chuckled. 'That has to be a present from Daisy.'

'She gave it to me last night.' Felix smiled back. 'And I handed her a box at the same time—containing exactly the same one.'

'Which goes to prove that you're the right one for her,' Nancy said. 'You see things the same way.'

Felix slipped the musical box back into his pocket.

'I suppose I ought to abide by tradition and wait for her inside.'

Diana Bell patted his shoulder, as if guessing what was worrying him. 'She'll be here, Felix,' she said softly. 'She turned Stuart down because he wasn't right for her. She said yes to you because you're the one. Nancy's right. You'll fit perfectly into our family.'

'Absolutely. He's one of us,' Ben said.

It warmed him that Daisy's family had taken him to their hearts so quickly. Just as his family had with her, once they'd got used to the idea of what Daisy did for a living.

'Let me do your buttonhole,' his mother said.

It was a single purple gerbera, flanked with fern. Just what he expected from Daisy.

Felix had no idea what she was going to wear. A white trouser-suit, maybe? Knowing that he wouldn't be able to pry a single word out of Annie or Alexis, he hadn't bothered trying, but even his sisters had closed ranks and refused to tell him. He knew that the brides-maids were wearing purple, but that was it.

'Come on, lad. We'll wait inside with you,' Bill said.

The tiny parish church was packed; the whole village seemed to have turned out to celebrate the wedding. Daisy was very much loved and, since he'd moved into the village, he was loved by extension. Everyone wanted to shake his hand, congratulate him and tell him that he couldn't have chosen a better bride, and it took him much longer than he'd expected to reach the altar.

'The bridesmaids are here,' Ben reported, and Felix's stomach knotted.

Then at last the organist played the first notes of the wedding processional from *The Sound of Music*, and

Felix turned round to see his bride walking down the aisle towards him.

She wasn't wearing trousers.

Her dress was stunning: a white dress that showed off her curves to perfection and had the spaghetti straps he loved her wearing; the skirt was flowing layers of tulle and organza. As she drew nearer he could see that the bodice was embroidered with tiny white daisies. Her hair was a mass of soft waves, just like the first night they'd had dinner together, and her face was hidden by a short veil attached to a tiara. It was only the second time Felix had ever seen her wear a dress, and she took his breath away.

He really hadn't expected her to go for something so traditional. Was this her way of telling him that she'd compromise?

He looked down automatically to check her feet. Her shoes were low-heeled...and adorned with purple daisies. And that was when he knew for certain it was the woman he loved walking down the aisle to him, not a woman trying to be someone she thought he'd love. His heart swelled within him. Trust her to go for the compromise: outwardly traditional but with the foundation very much her. Her four matrons of honour wore similar dresses in lilac and purple, and the two pageboys were dressed like him, in a tailcoat, lilac waistcoat and a purple cravat.

'You look amazing, and I love you so much,' he whispered as she joined him before the altar.

'So do you. And I love you, too, Felix,' she whispered back, then handed her simple sheaf of white roses and purple gerberas to Annie.

The ceremony was simple and beautiful. The sun was shining, the church was packed with everyone singing the hymns really loudly and Felix found himself wondering how he'd managed to get so lucky.

After the service, everyone pelted them with purple-and-ivory delphinium petals as they made their way through the lych gate to the carriage with its four white horses.

'Well, Ms Bell.' Daisy, being Daisy, had elected to keep her maiden name. 'You're the most beautiful bride I've ever seen,' Felix said softly as he helped her into the carriage.

'You don't look so bad yourself.' Daisy laced her fingers through his as he joined her. 'This has to be the best day of my life.'

'Mine, too,' Felix said.

The carriage driver took them to the fairground— which was officially closed for the day, as he and Daisy had decided that the first wedding reception celebrated there should be their own. Felix noted that the sign above the entrance was covered with dust-sheets. 'Daisy, is there a problem I should know about?'

She waved a hand at him. 'Minor detail. Don't worry about it.'

If she wasn't worried, then that was fine by him.

Once the photographs were over, they went over to the huge marquee that had been set up in the middle of the fairground gardens. 'I can't believe you managed to talk the hotel into catering this at such short notice, Felix,' she said.

'With you by my side,' he said, 'I can do anything. Though I will admit that I took our mothers with me, so they could help choose the menu and feel they were part of it.'

'Mr Fixit gets it right again,' she teased.

'And I believe that Mrs Fixit did the same thing with the dresses and the flowers.' He grinned. 'I did wonder if it was really you walking down the aisle to me. And then I saw your shoes and I knew.'

'They were hideously expensive.' She looked faintly guilty.

'I don't care. They're gorgeous. And I love that dress.' He kissed her shoulder, next to the spaghetti strap, and whispered, 'And I'm so looking forward to taking it off you tonight.'

'Felix.' Her eyes went unfocused and her voice was all breathy.

'Hold that thought, Boots,' he said softly. 'There's something I want to show you.' He led her over to the small table at the side of the top table.

Her eyes widened in surprise and pleasure as she saw the cake. 'Felix, that's…'

It wasn't often that his Daisy was lost for words. 'It's Shelley's finest chocolate cake,' he said. It was a three-tier circular cake, and round the outside Shelley had iced exact replicas of the three tiers of gallopers. The cake topper, made of spun sugar, was a bride and groom on a traditional fairground roundabout.

'I think I'm going to cry,' she said.

'Not on our wedding day, you're not.' He squeezed her hand. 'Now you know why I wouldn't tell you about the cake.'

'It's wonderful,' she said. 'And so are you.'

'I'll remind you of that next time I annoy you by tidying up.' He stole a kiss. 'Come on. Better sit down.'

After the meal, Ned Bell made the traditional father-of-the-bride speech, full of anecdotes. 'I'm not surprised she had wedding photographs taken on the gondola—the only surprise is that she didn't arrive at the church by steam train,' he teased.

Daisy laughed. 'Felix did ask the parish council if we could build a track down Church Street and they said no.'

'But luckily I *could* afford a carriage,' Felix added with a grin, 'or it would've been a tandem.'

'With a basket on the front for Titan,' Ned added. 'Welcome to the family, Felix. Ladies and gentlemen, I give you the bride and groom.'

And then it was Felix's turn to speak. He'd done public speaking before, and he was good at it. But his stomach was still in knots. Crazy. He stood up. 'Normally words aren't a problem for me, but today all I can think of is Daisy and how lucky I am to be married to her. She's everything to me. And a speech isn't enough to say it, so instead I'll do things her way.' He broke into an *a capella* version of 'I'd Do Anything'.

Daisy looked stunned at first, and then she joined in, her sweet voice the perfect counterpart to his.

Everyone laughed at the line where she asked him if he'd fight Bill, but there wasn't a dry eye in the house when they'd finished.

'The best man's speech is meant to be the one that everyone remembers,' Tristan Gisbourne said, standing up. 'But I can't top that. So I'll skip the words and get to the important bit. We're so pleased to welcome Daisy to our family. And I want to say a special thank you to Daisy because none of us have ever seen Felix look so happy. She's the one who's made that difference.' He lifted his glass. 'To Daisy.'

Felix's hand tightened round his bride's. 'He's right,' he whispered. 'You've made the difference.' Daisy had made him tell his family the truth about Tabitha, and their reaction had shown him that they really did love him for himself.

Once the reception was really underway—after they'd cut the cake, had the first dance and the fairground volunteers had gone to man the rides—Daisy tugged at his hand. 'Come with me. There's something I want to show you.' She led him to the fairground entrance. The sheets had been removed, and the sign was lit up.

Gisbourne & Bell.

Their names together, in lights.

Felix stared at it, completely taken aback. 'Daisy. I don't know what to say.'

'I made a vow today,' she said softly, 'in front of your family and mine, and the whole village. For richer, for poorer. Bill's signed his share of the fairground over to me as a wedding present. So your name needs to be there right next to mine.'

'Does it?' He took an envelope from the inside of his jacket pocket and handed it to her.

'What's this?'

'Wedding present. Me to you,' he said economically. She opened it, read it swiftly and stared at him. 'Felix?'

'I'm giving you my share of the fairground, too. So it's all yours.'

'Felix, I…' She kissed him hard. 'Thank you. Thank you so much. Though I didn't marry you for the fairground. You do know that, don't you?'

'I heard you say the words "love, honour and cherish" in church,' he said lightly. 'And I didn't hear the words, "for richer, for fairground".'

'That's a bit close to the bone,' she admonished him. 'But what I said about your name next to mine still stands. Because we're a team, and nothing's going to change that.'

'Felix Gisbourne and Daisy Bell,' he said. 'There's a nice ring to it.'

'Daisy and Felix Gisbourne,' she corrected.

He frowned. 'I thought you were keeping your name? Carrying on the tradition of the fairground?'

'I was. Until I thought about it, and I realised that I wanted all of you. Including your name.'

He shook his head. 'Daisy, don't feel you have to change for me.'

'I know you don't expect me to change to suit you. So I'm happy to take your name, Felix, to be your wife—because I want to.' She shrugged. 'Besides, it's less confusing for children if their parents have the same name.'

Felix sucked in a breath, joy flickering through his veins. 'Are you telling me you're...?'

'Pregnant? Not yet, though I think we might enjoy changing that. We'll have to practise a bit.' She smiled. 'You know what they say about biological clocks? You've set mine ticking.'

'Funny you should say that.' He kissed her gently. 'Because I have a confession to make. We're not cutting the top tier of our wedding cake today.'

'Why not?'

'Something you've taught me: traditions are important.'

As she caught his meaning, her eyes widened. 'The top tier's not chocolate, is it?'

'It's fruit cake,' he confirmed. 'Shelley says it will last, we can freeze it until we need it, and she'll re-ice it when the time comes.'

'Five months ago, if anyone had said I'd be talking about having babies, I would've laughed them out of my workshop,' Daisy said. 'And now…'

The look in her eyes made his heart skip a beat. 'Now, I think we stop talking,' he said. 'And we sneak off on honeymoon and I get the pleasure of carrying you over the threshold, before finding out exactly what Mrs Daisy Gisbourne is wearing under that delectable dress. And then,' he said with a grin, 'we start practising. Because we have some traditions to uphold.'

MILLS & BOON® ROMANCE

is proud to present

Jewels of the Desert

Deserts, diamonds and destiny!

The Kingdom of Quishari: two rulers, with hearts as
hard as the rugged landscape they reign over,
are in need of Desert Queens...

When they offer convenient proposals, will they
discover doing your duty doesn't have to
mean ignoring your heart?

Sheikh Rashid and his twin brother Sheikh Khalid
are looking for brides in...

ACCIDENTALLY THE SHEIKH'S WIFE

And

MARRYING THE SCARRED SHEIKH

by Barbara McMahon

in April 2010

MILLS & BOON® ROMANCE

is proud to present

THE BRIDES OF BELLA ROSA

Romance, rivalry and a family reunited

Lisa Firenze and Luca Casali's sibling rivalry has torn apart the quiet, sleepy Italian town of Monta Correnti for years…

Now, as the feud is handed down to their children, w history repeat itself? Can the next generation undc their parents' mistakes and reunite their families?

Or are there more secrets to be revealed…?

The saga begins in May 2010
with

BEAUTY AND THE RECLUSIVE PRINCE
by Raye Morgan

and

EXECUTIVE: EXPECTING TINY TWINS
by Barbara Hannay

Don't miss this fabulous sequel to
BRIDES OF BELLA LUCIA!

millsandboon.co.uk Community

Join Us!

e Community is the perfect place to meet and chat to
ndred spirits who love books and reading as much as
u do, but it's also the place to:

Get the inside scoop from authors about their latest books

Learn how to write a romance book with advice from our editors

Help us to continue publishing the best in women's fiction

Share your thoughts on the books we publish

Befriend other users

rums: Interact with each other as well as authors, edi-
rs and a whole host of other users worldwide.

ogs: Every registered community member has their
vn blog to tell the world what they're up to and what's
 their mind.

ok Challenge: We're aiming to read 5,000 books and
ve joined forces with The Reading Agency in our
augural Book Challenge.

ofile Page: Showcase yourself and keep a record of
ur recent community activity.

cial Networking: We've added buttons at the end of
ery post to share via digg, Facebook, Google, Yahoo,
chnorati and de.licio.us.

www.millsandboon.co.uk

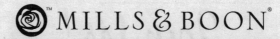